David's
Merry X-mas
2005

Love Aunt Barbie
&
Uncle George

Bought in Art Institute of Chicago

THIS BOOK BELONGS TO:

THE LITTLE BIG BOOK *for*

BOYS

Edited by
ALICE WONG &
LENA TABORI

Designed by
TIMOTHY SHANER &
CHRISTOPHER MEASOM

welcome
BOOKS
NEW YORK · SAN FRANCISCO

Published in 2003 by Welcome Books® • An imprint of Welcome Enterprises, Inc.
6 West 18 Street, New York, NY 10011 • (212) 989-3200; Fax (212) 989-3205
e-mail: info@welcomebooks.biz • www.welcomebooks.biz

Publisher: Lena Tabori   *Project Director:* Alice Wong
Designers: Timothy Shaner and Christopher Measom
Project Assistants: Jacinta O'Halloran, Lawrence Chesler, and Nicholas Liu
Activities and Recipes by Monique Peterson   *Heroines text by* David Cashion
Introductions to literary excerpts by Sara Baysinger
Additional text by Sara Baysinger, Rachel Hertz, and Deidra Garcia
Production Assitants: Kate Shaw and Naomi Irie   *Activities line illustrations by* Lawrence Chesler
Front jacket illustration by Nell Holt

Distributed to the trade in the U.S. and Canada by Andrews McMeel Distribution Services
Order Department and Customer Service (800) 943-9839 • Orders Only Fax (800) 943-9831

Copyright © 2003 by Welcome Enterprises, Inc.
Additional copyright information on page 352.

LIBRARY OF CONGRESS CATALOGING-IN-PUBLICATION DATA
The little big book for boys / edited by Alice Wong and Lena Tabori.
    p.cm. – (The Little big book series)
    Summary: An illustrated collection of literary excerpts, poems, songs, games,
recipes, miscellaneous facts, and activities for boys.
  ISBN 0-941807-70-3
    1. Boys—Literary collections. [1. Boys—Literary collections.] 1. Wong, Alice.
II. Tabori, Lena. III. Little big book (New York, N.Y.)

PZ5.L6854 2003
808.8'0083'41—dc21

                                                                    2002193360

Printed in Singapore

FIRST EDITION

3 5 7 9 10 8 6 4 2

Contents

Contents

Assorted Facts and Fun

Welcome

Welcome boys, **welcome!**
  You're in for a special treat.
This book is filled with the **coolest stuff**,
  To read, to do, to eat!

Ride a wild **Black Stallion**,
  Seek treasures with Tom and Huck.
Watch Arthur become a king—
  Was it magic or was it luck?

Visit a **chocolate** factory,
  Fight Hook with Peter Pan.
Find Lilliputians with Gulliver
  In a far and **distant land**.

Meet a boy named Fudge
  Who swallows his brother's turtle.
Be scared by the **Headless Horseman**—
  He's sure to make your blood curdle!

Gaze at the stars
And **dig in the dirt**;
Try questions and answers
Or **learn** how things work.

There are jokes and rhymes,
Songs and **games** galore—
No-Bake Treats and Monster Cookies,
Superheroes and **dinosaurs**.

Read all about **achievers**,
Heroes who paved the way.
Imagine, **dream**, and strive,
Maybe you'll be famous one day.

So, boys, **get ready** and go,
There is so much to do.
Just open to any page,
This book is **made for you**!

A boy is Truth with dirt on its face,

Beauty with a cut on its finger,

Wisdom with bubble gum on its hair,

And Hope of the future with a
frog in its pocket.

—Alan Marsh

Slow down, you move too fast.
You got to make the morning last.
Just kickin' down the cobblestones,
Lookin' for fun and Feelin' Groovy.

Hello lamppost, Whatcha knowin'
I've come to watch your flowers growin'
Ain'tcha got no rhymes for me?
Dootin' doo doo, Feelin' Groovy.

Got no deeds to do, no promises to keep.
I'm dappled and drowsy and ready to sleep.
Let the morning time drop all its petals on me.
Life, I love you,
All is groovy.

The 59th Street Bridge Song

(Feelin' Groovy)

by Paul Simon

Have you ever been bored, really bored? Have you ever had a day when you couldn't find anything interesting to do? Milo has. Not only that, but the boring days are piling up one on top of the other. Milo is convinced that there is nothing in the world that isn't a big waste of time. In fact, Milo regards "the process of seeking knowledge as the greatest waste of time of all." But just when he thinks life can't get any duller, Milo discovers a mysterious package in his bedroom. Partly because he is excited and partly because he has nothing better to do, Milo opens it. His world hasn't been dull since. Despite the huge success of *The Phantom Tollbooth* (1961) and his subsequent writing—including the classic *The Dot and the Line: A Romance in Lower Mathematics* (1963)—Norton Juster considers writing to be his second craft. His primary vocation is that of architect. He also serves as a professor emeritus at Hampshire College.

He looked glumly at all the things he owned. The books that were too much trouble to read, the tools he'd never learned to use, the small electric automobile he hadn't driven in months—or was it years?—and the hundreds of other games and toys, and bats and balls, and bits and pieces scattered around him. And then, to one side of the room, just next to the phonograph, he noticed something he had certainly never seen before.

Who could possibly have left such an enormous package and such a strange one? For, while it was not quite square, it was definitely not round, and for its size it was larger than almost any other big package of smaller dimension that he'd ever seen.

Attached to one side was a bright-blue enve-lope which said simply: "FOR MILO, WHO HAS PLENTY OF TIME."

Of course, if you've ever gotten a sur-prise package, you can imagine how puz-zled and excited Milo was; and if you've never gotten one, pay close attention, because someday you might.

"I don't think it's my birthday," he puzzled, "and Christmas must be months away, and I haven't been outstandingly good, or even good at all." (He had to admit this even to himself.) "Most probably I won't

The Phantom Tollbooth

by Norton Juster

like it anyway, but since I don't know where it came from, I can't possibly send it back." He thought about it for quite a while and then opened the envelope, but just to be polite.

"ONE GENUINE TURNPIKE TOLLBOOTH," it stated—and then it went on:

"EASILY ASSEMBLED AT HOME, AND FOR USE BY THOSE WHO HAVE NEVER TRAVELED IN LANDS BEYOND."

"Beyond what?" thought Milo as he continued to read.

"THIS PACKAGE CONTAINS THE FOLLOWING ITEMS:

"One (1) genuine turnpike tollbooth to be erected according to directions.

"Three (3) precautionary signs to be used in a precautionary fashion.

"Assorted coins for use in paying tolls.

"One (1) map, up to date and carefully drawn by master cartographers, depicting natural and man-made features.

"One (1) book of rules and traffic regulations, which may not be bent or broken."

And in smaller letters at the bottom it concluded:

"Most probably I won't like it anyway, but since I don't know where it came from, I can't possibly send it back."

'RESULTS ARE NOT GUARANTEED, BUT IF NOT PERFECTLY SATISFIED, YOUR WASTED TIME WILL BE REFUNDED."

Following the instructions, which told him to cut here, lift there, and fold back all around, he soon had the tollbooth unpacked and set up on its stand. He fitted the windows in place and attached the roof, which extended out on both sides, and fastened on the coin box. It was very much like the tollbooths he'd seen many times on family trips, except of course it was much smaller and purple.

"What a strange present," he thought to himself. "The least they could have done was to send a highway with it, for it's terribly impractical without one." But since, at the time, there was nothing else he wanted to play with, he set up the three signs,

SLOW DOWN APPROACHING TOLLBOOTH
PLEASE HAVE YOUR FARE READY
HAVE YOUR DESTINATION IN MIND

and slowly unfolded the map.

As the announcement stated, it was a beautiful map, in many colors, showing principal roads, rivers and seas, towns and cities, mountains and valleys, intersections and detours, and sites of outstanding interest both beautiful and historic.

"Dictionopolis," read Milo slowly when he saw what his finger had chosen. "Oh, well, I might as well go there as anywhere."

The only trouble was that Milo had never heard of any of the places it indicated, and even the names sounded most peculiar.

"I don't think there really is such a country," he concluded after studying it carefully. "Well, it doesn't matter anyway." And he closed his eyes and poked a finger at the map.

"Dictionopolis," read Milo slowly when he saw what his finger had chosen. "Oh, well, I might as well go there as anywhere."

He walked across the room and dusted the car off carefully. Then, taking the map and rule book with him, he hopped in and, for lack of anything better to do, drove slowly up to the tollbooth. As he deposited his coin and rolled past he remarked wistfully, "I do hope this is an interesting game, otherwise the afternoon will be so terribly dull."

21

We have tomorrow
Bright before us
Like a flame.

Yesterday
A night-gone thing,
A sun-down name.

And dawn-today
Broad arch above
   the road we came.

We march!

Youth

by Langston
Hughes

Blast Off!

Test the boundaries of speed and aerodynamics in your own backyard with rockets and race cars. Imagine that you're a NASA engineer and launch your own spaceship into orbit. Or perhaps you're a NASCAR racer testing how far your go-cart can travel on your own hot air. Get some friends together (and grown-ups, too) and see who'll break the next speed record!

Film Canister Rocket

Toilet paper tube, paper plate, tape, colored markers, construction paper, scissors, film canister, Alka-Seltzer tablet, water

NOTE: *This activity should be done outdoors with adult supervision.*

1. To make your rocket launcher, place one end of the toilet paper tube in the center of the paper plate. Tape it in place. Decorate your launcher with colored markers.
2. For the body of your rocket, cut a strip of construction paper about 5 x 4 inches. Wrap it around the film canister lengthwise, just underneath the lid. Tape it in place.
3. To make the top of your rocket, cut a circle out of construction paper about 4 inches in diameter. Make a single cut from the outside edge to the center of the circle.

Twist the circle into a cone shape and tape. Tape your cone to the top of the rocket body (the end opposite the film canister lid.)

4. Remove the lid to the film canister and drop in the Alka-Seltzer tablet and some water. Quickly reseal the film canister and position your rocket, lid down, in the launcher. The cone should be pointing toward the sky.
5. Stand back and prepare for launch!

Balloon Go-Cart Races

Clean Styrofoam meat or produce tray, scissors, four Styrofoam coffee cups, compass, four straight pins, flexi-straw, balloon, tape, ruler

1. For the base of your go-cart, trim the edges of the Styrofoam tray so that you have a flat base.
2. Cut the bases off the Styrofoam cups to use as wheels. Use your compass to find the center of each wheel, and mark it.

Attach the wheels to the base of your go-cart by pushing a straight pin into the center of each circle and then into the Styrofoam tray. These pins will serve as axles for your wheels, so be careful not to push them in too tightly.

3. Place the sipping end of the flexi-straw into the balloon opening. Tape it in place so that you can blow up the balloon through the other end of the straw. (First, you may want to blow the balloon up a few times to stretch the rubber. This will make it easier to blow up the balloon through the straw.)
4. Tape the middle of the straw lengthwise along the center of your go-cart.
5. Mark a starting point on a smooth surface for your racetrack. Gentlemen, on your marks . . .
6. Get set . . . Blow the balloon up through the straw. Pinch the straw end to prevent the air from releasing.
7. GO! Release the straw end and see how far your go-cart goes!

TIP: For best results, do this with a few friends.

GAMES for the ROAD

You've probably asked "How long till we get there?" more than once on a road trip. The next time you visit relatives or go on vacation, you can beat backseat boredom with a handful of games that don't require much more than your imagination. Now, getting there can be half the fun!

ALPHABET GAME

Players look for words that begin with each letter of the alphabet on road signs, billboards, buildings, train cars, or semi trucks. (License plate letters don't count.) When you find your A word, you must call it out so that no one else can claim it. Then you can go on to B, and so forth. (You can't call words out of order!) The tough letters are usually Q, X, and Z. So be sure to look for a Quick Mart after the RR Xing where there's a Speed Zone Ahead.

BOTTICELLI

One player thinks of a famous person or character. Everyone else takes turns asking yes or no questions. The player who guesses correctly wins the round and gets to lead the next one.

GOING ON A PICNIC

The first player recites the phrase, "I'm going on a picnic and I'm bringing _____." He or she fills in the blank with a word beginning with the letter A, such as APPLES. The second person recites the phrase and adds a B word: "I'm going on a picnic and I'm bringing APPLES and BANANAS. Each additional turn requires reciting the whole phrase and adding a new word that begins with the next letter of the alphabet. Whoever can't recite the growing list of items in proper order loses.

GEOGRAPHY

Players choose a category, such as cities, countries, rivers, or landmarks. The first player names something from that category. The next player must think of another name that starts with the last letter of the first name. For example, a city list could start: San Francisco, Omaha, Akron, New York, Kansas City. If a player can't think of another city, that person is out. The last player in the game wins.

GHOST

The first player says a letter. The next player must think of a word that starts with that letter and give a second letter. The object is for each player to add a letter without ending the word. (Two- and three-letter words don't count). For example, the letter called out is B. The next player adds U, thinking of BUSY. The third player adds M, thinking of BUMP. If the next player adds a P, he would lose the round. A smart choice would be the letter B (for bumble), to continue the round. The first player to end the word gets a letter G. A person who gets all the letters to spell GHOST loses.

*N*othing starts the day quite like a hot dish of eggs and hash browns. Frittatas are baked omelettes with just about anything in them that you like. In addition to the regular "suspects," try tossing in leftover spaghetti or fried rice! Next time you have tacos for dinner, save the leftovers for breakfast burritos! You can't get waffles as scrumptious as these variations. Make them on the weekend and freeze to toast later in the week for a quick and easy breakfast!

CRISPY WAFFLES

2 cups flour
1 tablespoon baking powder
2 cups milk
$^1/_3$ cup vegetable oil
2 eggs, separated

1. Preheat a waffle iron.
2. In a large bowl, mix flour and baking powder.
3. Add milk, oil, and egg yolks. Beat together with hand mixer until smooth.
4. In a separate bowl, whip egg whites until stiff. Gently fold into waffle batter.
5. Spoon about $^1/_3$ cup batter onto waffle grids. Close waffle iron and bake until golden and crisp, about 2 to 3 minutes.

TRY THESE VARIATIONS:

BANANA NUT

Mash one banana and fold into batter. Chop 1/2 cup pecans or walnuts and set aside. Pour batter onto waffle grid and then sprinkle a few teaspoons of nuts on top. Bake as directed.

BACON AND CHEESE

Fry 8 strips of bacon and crumble. Set aside. Grate $^1/_2$ cup cheddar cheese and fold into batter. Pour batter onto waffle grid and sprinkle crumbled bacon on top. Bake as directed.

CHOCOLATE PEANUT BUTTER

Fold 1 cup of chocolate chips into waffle batter and bake as directed. Spread peanut butter and honey on top of waffles and serve warm.

BREAKFAST BURRITOS

8 eggs
salt and pepper to taste
4 tortillas
1 tablespoon butter
$^1/_2$ cup cheddar or Monterey Jack cheese
1 avocado, diced
$^1/_4$ cup scallions, diced (optional)
4 strips bacon, fried and crumbled
8 teaspoons salsa

1. In a small bowl, beat eggs with a fork until blended. Add a dash of salt and pepper if desired. Meanwhile, heat oven to 250°F and warm tortillas on middle rack.
2. Melt butter in a skillet over medium heat.
3. Pour eggs into skillet and cook for 1 to 2 minutes. Gently stir with a spatula to let the uncooked egg settle at the bottom of the pan. Cook for another minute or until eggs are done to your liking.
4. Remove tortillas from oven and put onto plates. Divide the eggs evenly and spoon onto an outer third of each tortilla.
5. Add even amounts of cheese, avocado, scallions, bacon, and salsa on top of eggs.
6. To roll into burritos, fold in tortilla at sides, then roll tortilla edge with mixture toward other edge.

Makes 4 servings.

HEAVENLY HASH BROWNS

2 large baking potatoes
2 tablespoons butter
salt and pepper to taste

1. Scrub potatoes and grate them with the skins.
2. Melt butter in a large skillet over medium-high heat.
3. Add potatoes. Spread the potatoes evenly in the skillet and pat them down with a spatula. Sprinkle salt and pepper on top.
4. Fry potatoes until brown and crispy on the bottom, 5 to 8 minutes.
5. Flip the potatoes, in sections if necessary. Fry for another 5 minutes, or until brown and crispy. Serve hot with ketchup or salsa.

Makes 4 servings.

KITCHEN-SINK FRITTATAS

6 eggs
salt and pepper
2 cups leftovers
1 1/2 tablespoons butter

WESTERN: ham, cheese, peppers, green onions
GREEK: feta cheese, olives, plum tomatoes,
   spinach
SOUTHWEST: salsa, avocado, corn, Monterey
   Jack cheese, jalapeños, cilantro
ITALIAN: sausage, tomatoes, garlic, basil,
   Parmesan cheese
DOWN EAST: smoked salmon, dill, cream cheese
VEGGIE: zucchini, tomatoes, mozzarella cheese,
   broccoli, mushrooms

1. Preheat oven broiler.
2. Whisk eggs in a large bowl. Season with
   salt and pepper to taste.
3. Mix in all other ingredients except butter.
4. In a large ovenproof skillet, melt butter
   over medium heat.
5. Add egg mixture and cook until the
   bottom and edges are set, but eggs are
   still runny on top.
6. Remove skillet from stovetop and place
   under broiler. Broil about 3 minutes, until
   eggs are set and top is slightly browned.
7. Let frittata cool for a few minutes, then cut
   into wedges, and serve.

Makes 4 servings.

Tongue Twisters

Peter Piper picked a peck of pickled peppers
A peck of pickled peppers Peter Piper picked
If Peter Piper picked a peck of pickled peppers
Where's the peck of pickled peppers Peter Piper picked?

A flea and a fly flew up in a flue.
Said the flea, "Let us fly!"
Said the fly, "Let us flee!"
So they flew through a flaw in the flue!

A Tudor who tooted a flute
tried to tutor two tooters to toot.
Said the two to their tutor,
"Is it harder to toot
or to tutor two tooters to toot?"

I saw Esau kissing Kate,
And Kate saw I saw Esau,
And Esau saw that I saw Kate,
And Kate saw I saw Esau saw.

Oliver Oglethorp ogled an owl and an oyster.

Did Oliver Oglethorp ogle an owl and an oyster?

If Oliver Oglethorp ogled an owl and an oyster,

Where are the owl and the oyster Oliver Oglethorp ogled?

A Walk in the Woods

L̲earn how to discover true north without a compass, and how to figure out your average land speed. Knowing the pace at which you walk can help you estimate the time it will take you to complete a hike of known distance. As the Boy Scouts say, "Be prepared!"

FINDING TRUE NORTH

Stick, rope, two small pebbles

1. About 11 A.M., before the sun hits its highest point, push your stick straight into the ground.
2. Using the stick's shadow for the radius length, form a circle around your stick with the rope.
3. Place a pebble where the tip of the stick's shadow touches the edge of your circle.
4. Now wait. At about 1 P.M., the tip of the stick's shadow will touch the edge of the circle at another spot. Place your second pebble on that spot.
5. The imaginary straight line that connects the two pebbles is a true indication of an east-west line. The first pebble is the west end of the line. If you put your left foot on the first pebble, and your right foot on the second, you will be facing true north!

DEAD RECKONING

Tape measure, stopwatch, calculator

1. With a tape measure, mark two points on the ground 100 feet apart.
2. Use a stopwatch to count the number of seconds it takes you to walk from one marker to the next.
3. Walk the 100 feet a total of four times and find your average time by adding all the times together and dividing by four.
4. Then divide your average by 100. This will be your time (in seconds) per foot.
5. If you multiply that number by 60, you will have your average distance (in feet) per minute.
6. When you are walking, multiply your distance/minute ratio by the number of minutes you've been out. Then, if you divide that number by 5,280 (the number of feet in a mile), you'll know approximately how many miles you've gone.

37

NEIL ARMSTRONG (b. 1930) flew over two hundred different kinds of aircraft for the U.S. Navy in the 1950s before becoming the first man to walk on the moon. In July 1969, he was the commander of the Apollo 11 spacecraft, part of the first lunar landing mission. People all over the world watched Armstrong on their television sets as he put the first footprint on the moon and said, "That's one small step for a man, one giant leap for mankind."

DANIEL BOONE (1734–1820) grew up in the early days of America in the wilds of Pennsylvania and North Carolina. This great frontiersmen spent his childhood hunting, roaming the woods, and befriending Native Americans. He grew up to be a legendary trailblazer who helped create the Wilderness Road, which ran from eastern Virginia into Kentucky and beyond, and became the main route to the region then known as the West.

JACQUES COUSTEAU (1910–97) helped invent the Aqua-Lung, or SCUBA (self-contained underwater-breathing apparatus),

HEROES OF ADVENTURE & EXPLORATION

viewers discovered the sea world of sharks, fish, coral reefs, and sunken treasure for the first time. Over his lifetime, Cousteau traveled more than 1 million miles and made more than eighty expeditions worldwide.

LEWIS & CLARK are probably the most famous discovery team in American history. After serving as private secretary to Thomas Jefferson, Meriwether Lewis (1774–1809) was asked by the president to lead an exploration trek from St. Louis across uncharted land all the way to the Pacific Ocean. Remembering William Clark (1770–1838), a fellow soldier with a lot of frontier experience, Lewis asked his friend

to help him head up the Corps of Discovery expedition. They left in 1804 and returned in 1806, and their trip together was responsible for further exploration and settlement of a vast territory.

CHARLES A. LINDBERGH (1902–74) grew up on a farm in Minnesota but had a great talent for all things mechanical, so his mother and U.S. congressman father encouraged him to pursue his abilities. Eventually, he went to college and studied engineering and then went on to flight school. All that hard work and studying paid off when in 1927 he became the first person to fly solo across the Atlantic Ocean. He piloted his plane, the *Spirit of St. Louis*, the 3600 miles from New York to Paris in 33$\frac{1}{2}$ hours.

I'd like to be

under the sea

in an

octopus's garden

in the shade.

He'd let us in

knows where

we've been

in his octopus's

garden in the shade.

I'd ask my friends to come and see
An octopus's garden with me
I'd like to be under the sea
In an octopus's garden in the shade.

We would be warm below the storm
In our little hideaway beneath the waves
Resting our head on the seabed
In an octopus's garden near a cave.

We would sing and dance around
Because we know we can't be found.
I'd like to be under the sea
In an octopus's garden in the shade.

We would shout and swim about
The coral that lies beneath the waves
(Lies beneath the ocean waves).
Oh, what joy for every girl and boy
Knowing they're happy and they're safe
(Happy and they're safe).

We would be so happy, you and me;
No one there to tell us what to do.
I'd like to be under the sea
In a octopus's garden with you.

Peekaboo Periscope

You're a naval commander navigating uncharted seas. You're a spelunker exploring new cave passageways. You're a secret agent with special gadgets that let you peer around corners without being seen. All you need is a periscope, and you can be all of the above. Ask your mom, aunt, or big sister for some old cosmetic-case mirrors—and get ready to start looking at things from a new perspective!

Scissors, cardboard tubes (from wrapping paper, paper towels, or toilet paper), small mirrors, Scotch tape, black electrician's tape (optional)

1. Trim one end of a short cardboard tube at about a 45-degree angle. Do the same for a long tube. Make sure that the two trimmed tubes fit together perpendicularly so that they form a right angle.
2. Tape one edge of a mirror inside the trimmed opening of the long tube. Position the mirror at the joint between the long and short tubes so that it rests at a 45-degree angle opposite to the direction of the joint. Tape the other edge of the mirror inside the short tube. Tape the outsides of the tubes together so they form a 90-degree angle.
3. Repeat the same process for the opposite end of the long tube. You can face the short tubes in opposite directions, or you can build a U if you want to see what's behind you! Tape the second mirror in place so that it is parallel to the first.
4. Look in one end of your periscope, and you'll be able to see whatever the other end is facing. You can give your periscope a sleek look by wrapping it in electrician's tape.

Before it was a book, Peter Pan played to packed crowds in the London theater production called *Peter and Wendy* (1904). With the exception of a short interval during World War II, the play has run every Christmas since. The novel also first appeared under the title *Peter and Wendy*, but was not published until 1911. So how did Scottish writer Sir James Matthew Barrie (1860-1937) dream up the boy who refuses to grow up? Like Lewis Carroll, author of *Alice's Adventures in Wonderland*, Barrie had a real-life model for his main character in the form of young Peter Davies. Barrie "adopted" the five Davies boys as his companions, and would often make use of their observations and make-believe adventures in his stories. Peter Pan, too, wishes for some companions. So when he enters the nursery in search of his lost shadow, he convinces the Darling children to fly with him to Neverland, where they have many adventures together. The wicked Captain Hook means to spoil their fun, however. Will Peter finally defeat his archenemy and rescue Wendy Darling?

"**F**ling the girl overboard," cried Hook; and they made a rush at the figure in the cloak.

"There's none can save you now, missy," Mullins hissed jeeringly.

"There's one," replied the figure.

"Who's that?"

"Peter Pan the avenger!" came the terrible answer; and as he spoke Peter flung off his cloak. Then they all knew who 'twas that had been undoing them in the cabin, and twice Hook essayed to speak and twice he failed.
In that frightful moment I think his fierce heart broke.

At last he cried, "Cleave him to the brisket," but without conviction.

"Down, boys, and at them," Peter's voice rang out; and in another moment the clash of arms was resounding through the ship. Had the pirates kept together it is certain that they would have won; but the onset came when they were all unstrung, and they ran hither and thither, striking wildly, each thinking himself the last survivor of the crew. Man to man they were the stronger; but they fought on the defensive only, which enabled the boys to hunt in pairs and choose their quarry. Some of the miscreants leaped into the sea; others hid in dark recesses, where they were found by Slightly, who did not fight, but ran about

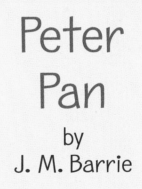

Peter Pan

by
J. M. Barrie

with a lantern which he flashed in their faces, so that they were half blinded and fell an easy prey to the reeking swords of the other boys. There was little sound to be heard but the clang of weapons, an occasional screech or splash, and Slightly monotonously counting—five—six—seven—eight—nine—ten—eleven.

I think all were gone when a group of savage boys surrounded Hook, who seemed to have a charmed life, as he kept them at bay in that circle of fire. They had done for his dogs, but this man alone seemed to be a match for them all. Again and again they closed upon him, and again and again he hewed a clear space. He had lifted up one boy with his hook, and was using him as a buckler, when another, who had just passed his sword through Mullins, sprang into the fray.

"Put up your swords, boys," cried the newcomer, "this man is mine."

"Proud and insolent youth," said Hook, "prepare to meet thy doom."

Thus suddenly Hook found himself face to face with Peter. The others drew back and formed a ring round them.

For long the two enemies looked at one another; Hook shuddering slightly, and Peter with the strange smile upon his face.

"So, Pan," said Hook at last, "this is all your doing."

"Ay, James Hook," came the stern answer, "it is all my doing."

"Proud and insolent youth," said Hook, "prepare to meet thy doom."

"Dark and sinister man," Peter answered, "have at thee."

Without more words they fell to and for a space there was no advantage to

47

either blade. Peter was a superb swordsman, and parried with dazzling rapidity; ever and anon he followed up a feint with a lunge that got past his foe's defense, but his shorter reach stood him in ill stead, and he could not drive the steel home. Hook, scarcely his inferior in brilliancy, but not quite so nimble in wrist play, forced him back by the weight of his onset, hoping suddenly to end all with a favorite thrust, taught him long ago by Barbecue at Rio; but to his astonishment he found this thrust turned aside again and again. Then he sought to close and give the quietus with his iron hook, which all this time had been pawing the air; but Peter doubled under it and, lunging fiercely, pierced him in the ribs. At sight of his own blood, whose peculiar color, you remember, was offensive to him, the sword fell from Hook's hand, and he was at Peter's mercy.

"Now!" cried all the boys, but with a magnificent gesture Peter invited his opponent to pick up his sword. Hook did so instantly, but with a tragic feeling that Peter was showing good form.

Hitherto he had thought it was some fiend fighting him, but darker suspicions assailed him now.

"Pan, who and what art thou?" he cried huskily.

"I'm youth, I'm joy," Peter answered at a venture, "I'm a little bird that has broken out of the egg."

This, of course, was nonsense; but it was

Seeing Peter slowly advancing upon him through the air with dagger poised, he sprang upon the bulwarks to cast himself into the sea.

proof to the unhappy Hook that Peter did not know in the least who or what he was, which is the very pinnacle of good form.

"To 't again," he cried despairingly.

He fought now like a human flail, and every sweep of that terrible sword would have severed in twain any man or boy who obstructed it; but Peter fluttered round him as if the very wind it made blew him out of the danger zone. And again and again he darted in and pricked.

"Pan, who and what art thou?" he cried huskily. "I'm youth, I'm joy," Peter answered. . . .

Hook was fighting now without hope. That passionate breast no longer asked for life; but for one boon it craved: to see Peter show bad form before it was cold forever.

Abandoning the fight he rushed into the powder magazine and fired it.

"In two minutes," he cried, "the ship will be blown to pieces."

Now, now, he thought, true form will show.

But Peter issued from the powder magazine with the shell in his hands, and calmly flung it overboard.

What sort of form was Hook himself showing? Misguided man though he was, we may be glad, without sympathizing with him, that in the end he was true to the traditions of his race. The other boys were flying around him now, flouting, scornful; and as he staggered about the deck striking up at them impotently, his mind was no longer with them; it was slouching in the playing fields of long ago, or being sent up for good, or watching the wallgame from a famous wall. And his shoes were right, and his waistcoat was right, and his tie was right, and his socks were right.

James Hook, thou not wholly unheroic figure, farewell.

For we have come to his last moment.

Seeing Peter slowly advancing upon him through the air with dagger poised, he sprang upon the bulwarks to cast himself into the sea. He did not know that the crocodile was waiting for him; for we purposely stopped the clock that this knowledge might be spared him: a little mark of respect from us at the end.

He had one last triumph, which I think we need not grudge him. As he stood on the bulwark looking over his shoulder at Peter gliding through the air, he invited him with a gesture to use his foot. It made Peter kick instead of stab.

At last Hook had got the boon for which he craved.

"Bad form," he cried jeeringly, and went content to the crocodile.

Thus perished James Hook.

FRISBEE GOLF

Aim and Toss

Number of players: two or more

What you need: a Frisbee, a large open area, paper and pencil for keeping score

Before play begins, everyone decides on what the "hole" will be—it can be a particular tree in the field, a pole, or whatever else serves as a large target. To make things interesting, the players also might decide on what "hazards" and obstacles to put on the way to the hole, like having to throw through an empty jungle gym, or a tunnel perhaps. Each player then takes a turn throwing the Frisbee as many times as it takes to reach the target. The fewer number of throws, the better. You can design numerous "holes" like these for an entire course.

TENNIS BALL ULTIMATE

Passing the Ball

Number of players: six or more

What you need: a tennis ball, a large open area

One team starts off as offense, while the other is defense. The goal of the game is to get the ball across your team's scoring line at one end of the field, but only by passing. Whoever has the ball is not allowed to move from his position until he passes it. Meanwhile, defending players can try to block or catch the throw, but they are not allowed to actually touch the thrower. If the

Fun & Games

thrower is unable to toss the ball after 10 seconds, or if the ball hits the ground or is intercepted, it goes to the other side.

TAG

You're it!

Number of players: unlimited

What you need: exuberance

REGULAR One of the players is "it," and he chases the others around, trying to tag them. Whoever gets tagged becomes the new "it."

BALL Same as regular tag, but instead of touching other players, "it" tosses a soft rubber ball to tag others.

BLOB Only one player starts off as "it," but as he tags other players, they join hands with "it," eventually making one massive "it" blob.

FREEZE Whoever gets tagged becomes "frozen," and has to stand perfectly still until he is touched by an unfrozen player.

POISON After someone is chosen as "it," the other players place their hands on their chests and start running. If a player gets tagged, he has to place a hand where he got touched, and now he's an "it" too. By the end of the game, you will have players running around with their hands touching their arms, legs, and backs. Whoever is tagged last becomes "it" for the next round.

EGG TOSS

Catch—please!

Number of players: four or more, in even numbers

What you need: a raw egg for every two players

Players pair off. Partners stand facing each other about 3 feet apart. Players on one side each hold an egg. The object of the game is to toss your egg to your partner, and hopefully, he or she will catch it. Players who drop their egg are out of the game. Players who catch their egg must take a big step back and toss the egg again. The last set of partners left in the game are the clean champions! (For a less messy though wetter version, you can use water balloons.)

Written more than a century ago, *The Jungle Book* (1894) is the story

of Mowgli, the man-cub, who is raised by a pack of wolves, and who

befriends memorable animals of the wild: Baloo, the wise and warm

brown bear, Bagheera, the silky black panther; Kaa, the cunning and

majestic python; and the nattering monkeys. These distinctly

personified creatures nurture young Mowgli and instruct him on the

laws of the jungle. Shere Khan, the sinister tiger, eventually threatens

Mowgli's idyllic existence. A highly respected author throughout his

lifetime, Kipling (1865-1936) nevertheless refused a number of honors,

including a knighthood and the Poet Laureateship. However, he did not

dare decline the highest tribute offered him: the Nobel Prize for Literature.

In 1907, he was the first English author to receive the award.

"Something is coming up hill," said Mother Wolf, twitching one ear. "Get ready."

The bushes rustled a little in the thicket, and Father Wolf dropped with his haunches under him, ready for his leap. Then, if you had been watching, you would have seen the most wonderful thing in the world—the wolf checked in mid-spring. He made his bound before he saw what it was he was jumping at, and then he tried to stop himself. The result was that he shot up straight into the air for four or five feet, landing almost where he left ground.

"Man!" he snapped. "A man's cub. Look!"

Directly in front of him, holding on by a low branch, stood a naked brown baby who could just walk—as soft and as dimpled a little atom as ever came to a wolf's cave at night. He looked up into Father Wolf's face, and laughed.

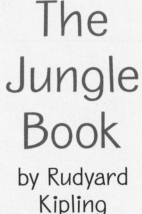

The Jungle Book

by Rudyard Kipling

"Is that a man's cub?" said Mother Wolf. "I have never seen one. Bring it here."

A wolf accustomed to moving his own cubs can, if necessary, mouth an egg without breaking it, and though Father Wolf's jaws closed right on the child's back, not a tooth even scratched the skin, as he laid it down among the cubs.

"How little! How naked, and—how bold!" said Mother Wolf, softly. The baby was pushing his way between the cubs to get close to the warm hide. "*Ahai!* He is

taking his meal with the others. And so this is a man's cub. Now, was there ever a wolf that could boast of a man's cub among her children?"

"I have heard now and again of such a thing, but never in our pack or in my time," said Father Wolf. "He is altogether without hair, and I could kill him with a touch of my foot. But see, he looks up and is not afraid."

The moonlight was blocked out of the mouth of the cave, for Shere Khan's great square head and shoulders were thrust into the entrance. Tabaqui, behind him, was squeaking: "My lord, my lord, it went in here!"

"Shere Khan does us great honor," said Father Wolf, but his eyes were very angry. "What does Shere Khan need?"

"My quarry. A man's cub went this way," said Shere Khan. "Its parents have run off. Give it to me."

Shere Khan had jumped at a woodcutters' campfire, as Father Wolf had said, and was furious from the pain of his burned feet. But Father Wolf knew that the mouth of the cave was too narrow for a tiger to come in by. Even where he was, Shere Khan's shoulders and fore paws were cramped for want of room, as a man's would be if he tried to fight in a barrel.

"The wolves are a free people," said Father Wolf. "They take orders from the head of the pack, and not from any striped cattle-

> "He is altogether without hair, and I could kill him with a touch of my foot. But see, he looks up and is not afraid."

59

killer. The man's cub is ours—to kill if we choose."

"Ye choose and ye do not choose! What talk is this of choosing? By the bull that I killed, am I to stand nosing into your dog's den for my fair dues? It is I, Shere Khan, who speak!"

The tiger's roar filled the cave with thunder. Mother Wolf shook herself clear of the cubs and sprang forward, her eyes, like two green moons in the darkness, facing the blazing eyes of Shere Khan.

"And it is I, Raksha (the Demon), who answer. The man's cub is mine, Lungri—mine to me! He shall not be killed. He shall live to run with the pack and to hunt with the pack; and in the end, look you, hunter of little naked cubs—frog-eater—fish-killer—he shall hunt *thee!* Now get hence, or by the sambur that I killed (I eat no starved cattle), back thou goest to thy mother, burned beast of the jungle, lamer than ever thou camest into the world! Go!"

Father Wolf looked on amazed. He had almost forgotten the days when he won Mother Wolf in fair fight from five other wolves, when she ran in the pack and was not called the Demon for compliment's sake. Shere Khan might have faced Father Wolf, but he could not stand up against Mother Wolf, for he knew that where he was she had all the advantage of the ground, and would fight to the death. So he backed out of the cave-mouth growling and when he was clear he shouted:

"Each dog barks in his own yard! We will see what the pack will say to this fostering of man-cubs. The cub

> The tiger's roar filled the cave with thunder.

is mine, and to my teeth he will come in the end, O bushtailed thieves!"

Mother Wolf threw herself down panting among the cubs, and Father Wolf said to her gravely:

"Shere Khan speaks this much truth. The cub must be shown to the pack. Wilt thou still keep him, Mother?"

"Keep him!" she gasped. "He came naked, by night, alone and very hungry; yet he was not afraid! Look, he has pushed one of my babes to one side already. And that lame butcher would have killed him and would have run off to the Wainganga while the villagers here hunted through all our lairs in revenge! Keep him? Assuredly I will keep him. Lie still, little frog. O thou Mowgli—for Mowgli the Frog I will call thee—the time will come when thou wilt hunt Shere Khan as he has hunted thee."

"The cub is mine, and to my teeth he will come in the end, O bushtailed thieves!"

61

A Song of Greatness

A Chippewa Indian Song
Transcribed by
Mary Austin

When I hear the old men
Telling of heroes,
Telling of great deeds
Of ancient days,
When I hear them telling,
Then I think within me
I too am one of these.

When I hear the people
Praising great ones,
Then I know that I too
Shall be esteemed,
I too when my time comes
Shall do mightily.

YOUGEST RELAY TEAM TO SWIM THE CHANNEL

The youngest six-member relay team to cross the English Channel was the Thane District AAA team from Mumbai (Bombay), India, who swam from Shakespeare Beach, Dover, Kent, UK, to Cap Gris-Nez, France, in 11 hrs. 23 mins. on Aug. 12, 1996. The team members were Kaveri Thakur (13), Rahul Modi (13), Daniel Reuben (13), Gunjan Parulkar (14), Rashmi Sansare (14), and Siddesh Parab (14).

YOUGEST CHAMPION

The youngest successful competitor in a world title event was a French boy, whose name is not recorded, who coxed the Netherlands' Olympic pair in the rowing competition at Paris, France, on Aug. 26 1900. He was not more than 10 and may have been as young as 7.

Young Champions

YOUNGEST PLAYER TO SCORE A HAT TRICK The youngest scorer of a hat trick (3 goals in a game) in UK football was Tommy Lawton, age 17 years, 5 days, for Burnley v. Spurs at Turf Moor on Oct. 10, 1936. The youngest player to score a hat trick in the Premiership was Michael Owen, (UK), age 18 years, 62 days, for Liverpool v. Sheffield on Wednesday, Feb. 14, 1998.

YOUNGEST ATHLETICS WORLD-RECORD HOLDER The youngest male to set an official world record is Thomas Ray (UK), who was 17 years, 198 days when he set a pole-vault record of 11 ft 2.75 in (3.42m) on Sept. 19, 1879.

YOUNGEST CONCRETE BLOCK BREAKER David Chu Tan (Germany), trained by his father—a martial arts master—was 11 years old when he managed to break 24 concrete blocks with his head in 30 seconds while doing a forward back flip—one for every two blocks. He set this record on Dec. 20, 2000. David's father had been training David since he was a small child.

*T*his Big Bad Burger is so good—it's bad! It's sure to satisfy any appetite. For the best grilled-cheese sandwich ever, try this classic French variation, called a Croque Monsieur. The secret is a hot slice of ham in the middle of the melted cheese. Yum! Wraps make it easy to add just about anything to a sandwich, without food falling out the sides as you eat. But if you have a mess of an appetite, you must make the ultimate hero. Just a word of warning: You may need to invite the football team over to help you finish it!

BIG BAD BURGER

6 ounces ground beef
1 egg yolk
1 tablespoon cooked spinach, well drained and chopped
1 teaspoon grated onion
salt and freshly ground black pepper
1 tablespoon grated Swiss or cheddar cheese
mayonnaise, to taste
ketchup, to taste
1 wholewheat roll or hamburger bun
2 lettuce leaves, cleaned and chopped
2 slices ripe tomato

1. Preheat broiler.
2. In a large bowl, combine beef, egg yolk, spinach, onion, and salt and pepper and mix well.
3. Form three quarters of the meat mixture into a patty, and set the remaining mixture aside.
4. Make an indentation in the center of the patty, and fill it with the cheese. Cover the cheese with the remaining meat mixture, and form a finished patty.
5. Broil the patty for $2^1/_2$ to 3 minutes on each side for a juicy rare burger—or broil longer to your preference.
6. Spread mayonnaise and ketchup on each side of the wholewheat roll or toasted bun. Place the burger on the bottom half, top it with lettuce and tomato slices, and cover it with the other half of the bun.

Makes 1 serving.

CROQUE MONSIEUR

4 slices bread
2 ounces Swiss cheese, thinly sliced
2 ounces Canadian bacon, thinly sliced
1^1/$_2$ tablespoons butter

1. Cover two slices of bread with ^{1}/$_2$ ounce of cheese. Layer 1 ounce of Canadian bacon, then top with remaining cheese. Cover with bread slices.
2. Melt butter in skillet over medium heat.
3. Fry sandwiches, pressing down gently with spatula, until browned on the bottom. Turn sandwiches over and fry until second side is browned.
4. Remove from skillet and cut diagonally to make triangle halves. Serve warm.

Makes 2 sandwiches.

IT'S A WRAP

Try these combinations on a plain or flavored tortilla. To wrap, fold the bottom of the tortilla about a fourth of the way up, then fold the left side over the middle and the right side over the left. Then finish rolling, pick it up, and sink your teeth into it!

TURKEY BLT

^{1}/$_8$ pound thinly sliced turkey
2 slices bacon, cooked
2–3 slices tomato
^{1}/$_4$ cup shredded lettuce
1 tablespoon creamy peppercorn or ranch dressing

VEGGIE SUPREME

1 tablespoon herbed cream cheese
^{1}/$_4$ avocado, sliced
^{1}/$_4$ yellow pepper, cut into strips
2–3 slices tomato
2–3 slices red onion
4–6 spinach leaves
2 tablespoons grated carrot
2 tablespoons alfalfa sprouts

BIG BITES

TUNA SALAD

2 leaves romaine lettuce
Blend: 3 ounces tuna fish, 1 diced pickle,
1 tablespoon mayonnaise, $1/2$ teaspoon
lemon juice

REUBEN

2 slices corned beef
1 slice Swiss cheese
3 tablespoons sauerkraut
1 tablespoon Thousand Island dressing

SKY-HIGH & MILE-LONG HERO

Slice a loaf of French bread and spread butter, mayonnaise, and mustard on both halves. Then add as much of the following ingredients as you like.

- Cheddar cheese
- Swiss cheese
- Monterey Jack cheese
- Fontina cheese
- Parmesan cheese
- mozzarella cheese
- salami
- bologna

- mortadella
- meatballs
- ham
- bacon
- fried eggs
- tomato slices
- avocado slices or guacamole
- green pepper strips

- pineapple slices
- onion rings
- pickle slices
- olives
- cole slaw
- shredded lettuce
- spinach leaves
- green chilies

69

It Couldn't Be Done

by Edgar A. Guest

Somebody said that it couldn't be done,
    But he with a chuckle replied
That "maybe it couldn't," but he would be one
    Who wouldn't say so till he'd tried.
So he buckled right in with the trace of a grin
    On his face. If he worried he hid it.
He started to sing as he tackled the thing
    That couldn't be done, and he did it.

Somebody scoffed: "Oh, you'll never do that;
    At least no one ever has done it";
But he took off his coat and he took off his hat,
    And the first thing we knew he'd begun it.
With a lift of his chin and a bit of a grin,
    Without any doubting or quiddit,
He started to sing as he tackled the thing
    That couldn't be done, and he did it.

There are thousands to tell you it cannot be done,
    There are thousands to prophesy failure;
There are thousands to point out to you, one by one,
    The dangers that wait to assail you.
But just buckle in with a bit of a grin,
    Just take off your coat and go to it;
Just start to sing as you tackle the thing
    That "cannot be done," and you'll do it.

Airplane

Humans have always dreamed of flying. Beginning in 1505, Leonardo da Vinci (1452-1519) studied the flight of birds and tinkered with ideas for flying machines. So how did we get from da Vinci's drawings to our 747 jet planes? How can a heavier-than-air (as much as 870,000 pounds at takeoff) vehicle with a carrying capacity of 600 plus people get off the runway?

The most basic (yet troublesome) principle to grasp about flying is that air has atmosphere—air is a gas is a liquid. This is important to understand because it is the constant pressure of this "liquid" around the plane, and particularly the wings, that keeps a plane aloft.

There are four basic aerodynamic forces. They are lift, weight, thrust, and drag. *Lift* is generated when air particles split at the edge of the wing, either going over or under the wing.

Because of the curved shape on top of the wing, the particles traveling over the top travel faster than those at the bottom. Faster-moving air has lower pressure than slow-moving air. The greater pressure under the wing forces the wing up. When lift surpasses weight, the aircraft "lifts off."

Like lift and weight, thrust and drag work together. The propellers or jet engines of a plane create thrust. Like a household fan, air is moved over the blades. Air's resistance to an object moving through it creates drag. Just as your hand feels pressure when you hold it out of the window of a moving car, so a plane "feels" pressure as it moves through the air. When there is more thrust than drag on a plane, it speeds up.

Hot-Air Balloon

It looks like a huge parachute attached to a basket, so what keeps a hot-air balloon from falling to the ground? Well, the huge piece of synthetic fabric shaped like a bulb is called an *envelope*. A balloon is also equipped with a burner and a basket. When not in use, a hot-air balloon's envelope is limp. To get the balloon to fly, the operator fills the envelope with hot air using the propane gas in the burner. Once the balloon is upright, the passengers—some balloons can fly with up to ten—pile into the basket. The operator then continues to heat the air inside the envelope (to about 100° C) until it expands enough to force a quarter of the total air out the base of the envelope. When the weight of the balloon is reduced to less than its *upthrust*, it takes off. The operator has no real means to steer the balloon, but can keep it at a constant height with intermittent blasts from the burner. The balloon drifts with the wind until the burner is cut off. Air in the envelope cools and contracts, and more cool air is able to enter into the envelope. This weighs the balloon down, causing it to descend. The operator uses short bursts of the burner to create a soft landing.

SCIENCE TRICKS

Science can feel like magic much of the time. Put on a "magic" show for your friends with these great experiments! They will think you are a talented magician or a genius!

Magnetic Fields

iron filings, three magnets (round, bar, and u-shaped), three sheets of paper, paper cup

1. Place your iron filings in the paper cup.
2. Set the three magnets out on a table with a sheet of paper covering each.
3. Sprinkle each paper with iron filings and watch them quickly form patterns on the paper.

PRINCIPLES AT WORK: The iron filings are pulled into the magnetic field of the respective magnets. The closer the filings are to the magnet, the more force is exerted on them. For the bar and *u*-shaped magnets, the force is strongest at the ends, so more filings should gather there. The force is equal around all the edges of the round magnet, so the filings will create a circular pattern.

Pendulum

tennis ball, string (approximately 6 feet long), thumbtack

1. Tie one end of your string tightly around the tennis ball. Attach the other end to the ceiling (at least 4 feet from the nearest wall) with the thumbtack. You may alternately tie the other end to a tree branch.
2. Ask your friend to hold the tennis ball so that it is just touching the tip of his or her nose and walk backward until the the string is taut.
3. Release the ball to begin the pendulum motion.

4. The ball will swing out and back but it will not touch your friend. It'll just make him flinch!

PRINCIPLES AT WORK: Pendulums work on the principle of periodic motion. This means that theoretically, the ball should continue to swing out and back, forever, touching the tip of your friends nose each time. However, gravity, the friction of the string and its attach point, and the air resistance against the ball and string cause the pendulum to slow with each swing until it eventually stops.

Surface Tension
strainer, cooking oil, shallow bowl, small glass of water

1. Coat the wire mesh of your strainer with cooking oil either by pouring it through the strainer into the bowl or dipping the strainer into a small bowl of oil.
2. Holding the coated strainer over the sink, carefully add the glass of water. The water should stay inside of the strainer.
3. Ask your friend to touch the underside of the strainer with their fingers or a toothpick. The water should run out of the strainer into the sink.

PRINCIPLES AT WORK: The water stays inside the strainer at first because the oil coats the rough wire and creates a "skin" of surface tension. The molecules of water already have a very strong attraction, and the oil helps reinforce the attraction to fight against gravity and the sharp edges of the wire mesh. The surface tension bonds are broken once your friend's hand or toothpick breaks the surface of the oil.

GEORGE WASHINGTON CARVER
(1864–1943) was born a slave on a Missouri
plantation, and because of this, he never went
to elementary school. Instead, after he finished his chores, he would go into the woods,
do his own experiments, and teach himself
about the natural world. Later, when he was a
free man, Carver was the first African
American to graduate from Iowa State
University. His studies in farming led him to
discover 325 uses for peanuts (including
peanut butter) and over 100 uses for sweet
potatoes. Carver also created better ways for
farmers to work with soil and crops. These
methods are still used today.

THOMAS ALVA EDISON (1847–1931)
was probably the greatest and most
productive inventor of his time. While
Edison was growing up in Michigan, his
teacher complained that he asked too
many questions. Young Tom's parents
supported his curiosity, and he set up his
first science laboratory in their basement
when he was ten. Edison went on to hold
patents on over a thousand inventions,
including the phonograph and the light bulb,
and he even helped to create motion pictures.

ALBERT EINSTEIN (1879–1955) is generally
thought of as one of the greatest scientists in
the modern world. Einstein was born in
Germany, but brought his knowledge of

THEORY OF RELATIVITY

OH YEAH!

physics to America in the 1930s. His most famous contribution is the theory of relativity, which has to do with time, space, and the motion of objects. While Einstein's famous $E=mc^2$ equation about energy and atoms was used by scientists in the development of the nuclear bomb, this Nobel Prize-winner always worked for peace.

BENJAMIN FRANKLIN (1706–90) did much more than fly a kite in a storm and discover that lightning contains electricity: He was a diplomat, printer, philosopher, and writer, in addition to being an inventor and scientist. The list of his inventions includes bifocal eyeglasses, the lightning rod, the odometer, and the iron furnace stove, a.k.a. the Franklin stove. Toward the end of his life, he made one of his greatest contributions: signing the Declaration of Independence.

STEPHEN HAWKING (b. 1942) has not let a disease that confines him to a wheelchair and forces him to use a computerized voice box keep him from being a brilliant scientist. This English genius actually provided mathematical evidence to back up the famous big bang theory, which offers an explanation of how the universe began. His work on black holes and the connection between space and time also is celebrated.

ISAAC NEWTON (1642–1727) achieved gigantic breakthroughs in mathematics (inventing the mathematical field of calculus) and in ideas relating to color. However, Newton is probably most famous for observing an apple as it fell from a tree. From just sitting under a tree when its fruit fell from the branch, he discovered the force of gravity, and the world has never been the same.

Bugs, Bugs, Bugs

The earth is crawling with some 8 million species of bugs—that's more than any other creature on the planet. And we're still counting! Scientists in Southern Africa recently discovered an entirely new order of insect. Nicknamed the "gladiator bug", it looks something like a mixture of grasshopper, stick insect, and mantis. What if the next new breed of bug lives in your backyard? There's only one way to find out: Grab a net, put on your bug-eyes, and go!

Bug Catcher

Some bugs can be pretty hard to catch without a net. Others are so delicate that we'd squish them if we tried to pick them up. With a good bug net, you can catch all kinds of flyers, buzzers, crawlers, and creepers. No insect expedition is complete without one.

Wire hanger, large plastic bag, wooden dowel or old broom handle, duct tape, tape, screwdriver, hammer, large jar with lid

1. Carefully untwist and bend the coat hanger into a loop no larger than the opening of your plastic bag.
2. Wrap the ends around the end of the broom handle and secure with duct tape.
3. Use tape to fit the edge of the plastic bag around the coat hanger.
4. Use a screwdriver and hammer to poke holes in the jar lid for ventilation. Now you're ready to buzz off for a bug hunt!

Insect Incubator

One of the best ways to learn about bug life is by watching them hatch and grow. Look for places insects might lay eggs, such as trees, shrubs, or underneath moss or bark. Check a local field guide to determine what bugs may be in your area and to help identify their eggs. Be careful not to disturb the eggs once you find them. Gather the twigs, leaves, or bark on which the eggs have been laid. Collect additional similar vegetation that can provide nutrition for the insects once they hatch.

Egg-laden twigs, cotton, small glass bottle, dirt, water, flowerpot (4¹/₂ inches in diameter), 2-liter plastic soda bottle, scissors, cheesecloth, rubber band

1. Pack the ends of the egg-laden twigs and fresh twigs in cotton and place them in a small bottle of water. Sprinkle a light layer of dirt on top of the water.

2. Place the bottle neck-deep in a flowerpot with dirt. If you've found eggs underneath bark or moss, place those on top of the dirt next to the bottle.

3. You can turn the plastic bottle into a see-through "chimney." Ask an adult to help you cut the neck and the bottom 2 inches off your bottle and discard. Then fit the wider end of the bottle inside the edge of the flowerpot. It should fit snugly.

4. Cover the top of the plastic bottle with cheesecloth and secure in place using the rubber band.

5. Now watch what happens! Depending on the species of eggs, the hatching process may take anywhere from a few days to a few weeks. Keep a journal to record your findings. After the bugs have hatched, take the incubator back to the place where you found the eggs, and carefully release them into the wild.

Dream on, little cowboy,
of rocket ships and Mars,
of sunny days and Willie Mays
and chocolate bars.
Dream on, little cowboy,
dream while you can,
of big green frogs
and puppy dogs,
and castles in the sand.

Are You Lucky?

Don't break a mirror – 7 years of bad luck!

*D*o you flinch with a black cat crosses your path? Do you find yourself staring at the sidewalk, tiptoeing over the cracks? Do you carry a rabbit's foot in your pocket? Boy, you're superstitious. Still not lucky enough? Here are more things to try. Good luck!

● Get out of bed on the same side you got in to avoid bad luck ●

Cross your fingers ● Find a four-leaf clover ● Carry an acorn

● Spit on a new bat for good luck before using it for the first time ●

Hang a horseshoe above your doorway ● Don't walk under a ladder

● Pick up a penny if it's heads side up, don't touch if it's tails up!

● If you spill salt, throw it over your left shoulder to avoid bad luck

● Don't open an umbrella in the house ● For a lucky fishing

day throw back the first fish you catch ●

Don't leave your shoes upside down!

Outside Or Underneath?

by Shel Silverstein

Bob bought a hundred-dollar suit
But couldn't afford any underwear.
Says he, "If your outside looks real good
No one will know what's under there."

Jack bought some hundred-dollar shorts
But wore a suit with rips and tears.
Says he, "It won't matter what people see
As long as I know what's under there."

Tom bought a flute and a box of crayons,
Some bread and cheese and a golden pear.
And as for his suit or his underwear
He doesn't think about them much... or care.

The Search

by Shel Silverstein

I went to find the pot of gold
That's waiting where the rainbow ends.
I searched and searched and searched
    and searched
And searched and searched, and then—
There it was, deep in the grass,
Under an old and twisty bough.
It's mine, it's mine, it's mine at last....
What do I search for now?

Map It!

Plan a treasure hunt, bury a time capsule, or stake out a clubhouse. How are you going to tell your friends where to go? Make a map, of course! You don't have to be a cartographer to make a good sketch map. Whether you want to chart an area of town or a route in the country, you can incorporate common symbols to indicate natural or man-made structures, landmarks, or topography. Like every good mapmaker, be sure to add personal knowledge about the area, such as the barking dog in the used-car lot, the house with the yummiest homemade cookies, or the creek with the most tadpoles.

Sketchbook, pencil, compass, graph paper

1. Choose the area you'd like to include in your map. Then find a good reference point, like a tree, a hill, or a building, from which you can see a good portion of the area you want to map out.
2. Take some time to observe the land. Make notes in your sketchbook about your location and the roads, landmarks, and structures that are visible from your viewpoint. Use your compass to find north and include that in your sketch.
3. If possible, go to two or three different points of reference and make additional sketches. Then, using your graph paper, make a composite map from your various sketches. You'll be surprised how much you can learn about an area by mapping it!

Use these basic topographical symbols when creating your map:

Corn and Cultivated Land

Buildings — General

Palm and Palmetto

Schoolhouse

Pack Trail

Railroad — Any kind

Church

Cemetery

Ford (Wading Place)

Foot Bridge

Bridge

Lock (Point upstream)

Lake

Good Motor Road

Poor Motor Road

Town

Windmill

Quarry — Mine

Woods — Broad leaves

Woods — Pines, etc.

Grassland

Marsh

Mark Twain (1835-1910), born Samuel Langhorne Clemens, grew up in a poor family in Hannibal, Missouri. His father died when he was just twelve years old, and so Samuel was forced to abandon his childhood to help support his family. His first jobs included a printer's apprentice, a newspaper writer, and a pilot of a steamship on the Mississippi. This last occupation provided much of the material for his most famous books, *The Adventures of Tom Sawyer* and *The Adventures of Huckleberry Finn*. It was also the inspiration for his pen name. (His shipmates would shout "mark twain" to measure the depth of the river—twain equaling two fathoms.) Twain's use of language—particularly with regard to dialogue—uniquely captures the rich landscape and voice of the American frontier. His deep understanding of human nature infuses his stories with a realism that sets them apart. *The Story of Tom Sawyer*, which details his exploits with his band of friends, was published in 1876. Here we find merrily mischievous Tom joining forces with his lawless companion Huckleberry Finn to search for hidden treasure.

There comes a time in every rightly constructed boy's life when he has a raging desire to go somewhere and dig for hidden treasure. This desire suddenly came upon Tom one day. He sallied out to find Joe Harper, but failed of success. Next he sought Ben Rogers; he had gone fishing. Presently he stumbled upon Huck Finn the Red-handed. Huck would answer. Tom took him to a private place, and opened the matter to him confidentially. Huck was willing. Huck was always willing to take a hand in any enterprise that offered entertainment and required no capital, for he had a troublesome superabundance of that sort of time which is *not* money.

"Where'll we dig?" said Huck.

"Oh, 'most anywhere."

"Why, is it hid all around?"

"No, indeed it ain't. It's hid in mighty particular places, Huck—sometimes on islands, sometimes in rotten chests under the end of a limb of an old dead tree, just where the shadow falls at midnight; but mostly under the floor in ha'nted houses."

"Who hides it?"

"Why, robbers, of course— who'd you reckon? Sunday-school sup'rintendents?"

"I don't know. If it was mine I wouldn't hide it; I'd spend it and have a good time."

The Adventures of Tom Sawyer

by Mark Twain

"So would I; but robbers don't do that way, they always hide it and leave it there."

"Don't they come after it any more?"

"No, they think they will, but they generally forget the marks, or else they die. Anyway it lays there a long time and gets rusty; and by-and-by somebody finds an old yellow paper that tells how to find the marks—a paper that's got to be ciphered over about a week because it's mostly signs and hy'roglyphics."

"Hyro—which?"

"Hy'roglyphics—pictures and things, you know, that don't seem to mean anything."

"Have you got one of them papers, Tom?"

"No."

"Well, then, how you going to find out the marks?"

"I don't want any marks. They always bury it under a ha'nted house, or on an island, or under a dead tree that's got one limb sticking out. Well, we've tried Jackson's Island a lit- tle, and we can try it again sometime; and there's the old ha'nted house up the Still-House branch, and there's lots of dead-limb trees—dead loads of 'em."

"Is it under all of them?"

"How you talk! No!"

"Then how you going to know which one to go for?"

"Go for all of 'em."

"Why, Tom, it'll take all summer."

"They always bury it under a ha'nted house, or on an island, or under a dead tree that's got one limb sticking out."

"Well, what of that? Suppose you find a brass pot with a hundred dollars in it, all rusty and gay, or a rotten chest full of di'monds. How's that?"

Huck's eyes glowed.

"That's bully, plenty bully enough for me. Just you gimme the hundred dollars, and I don't want no di'monds."

"All right. But I bet you *I* ain't going to throw off on di'monds. Some of 'em's worth twenty dollars apiece. There ain't any, hardly, but's worth six bits or a dollar."

"No! Is that so?"

"Cert'nly—anybody'll tell you so. Hain't you ever seen one, Huck?"

"Not as I remember."

"Oh, kings have slathers of them."

"Well, I don't know no kings, Tom."

"I reckon you don't. But if you was to go to Europe you'd see a raft of 'em hopping around."

"Do they hop?"

"Hop?—your granny! No!"

"Well, what did you say they did for?"

"Shucks! I only meant you'd *see* 'em—scat-tered around, you know, in a kind of general way. Like that old hump-backed Richard."

"Richard! What's his other name?"

"He didn't have any other name. Kings don't have any but a given name."

"No?"

"But they don't."

So they got a crippled pick and a shovel, and set out on their three-mile tramp.

"Well, if they like it, Tom, all right; but I don't want to be a king and have only just a given name, like a nigger. But say—where you going to dig first?"

"Well, I don't know. S'pose we tackle that old dead limb tree on the hill t'other side of Still-House branch?"

"I'm agreed."

So they got a crippled pick and a shovel, and set out on their three-mile tramp. They arrived hot and panting, and threw themselves down in the shade of a neighboring elm to rest and have a smoke.

"I like this," said Tom.

"So do I."

"Say, Huck, if we find a treasure here, what you going to do with your share?"

"Well, I'll have a pie and a glass of soda every day, and I'll go to every circus that comes along. I'll bet I'll have a gay time."

"Well, ain't you going to save any of it?"

"Save it? What for?"

"Why, so as to have something to live on by-and-by."

"Oh, that ain't any use. Pap would come back to thish yer town some day and get his claws on it if I didn't hurry up, and I tell you he'd clean it out pretty quick. What you going to do with yourn, Tom?"

"I'm going to buy a new drum, and a sure-'nough sword, and a red necktie, and a bull-pup, and get married."

"Married!"

"That's it."

"Tom, you—why, you ain't in your right mind."

You are a human boy, my young friend.
A human boy!
O running stream of sparkling joy,
To be a soaring human boy!

—Charles Dickens

Build a Lean-to

Whether you're hiking as far as a mountain lake or as close as your backyard, you can up the adventure ante by making your own shelter. Lean-tos are easy to construct and a fun way to practice your wilderness survival skills. So grab a friend and get ready for the outdoors—come rain, snow, or wind!

Poles (you can use tent poles, broomsticks or whatever is easily available), rope, branches, boughs, canvas or tarp (optional)

1. Pick the site where you'd like to build your lean-to and check the wind direction. To shelter you, the back of your lean-to must face the wind.
2. Clear a level spot for your shelter. Look for a natural structure that might serve as a main support for your lean-to, such as some trees or a large boulder. If a natural support isn't available, you can make a frame by anchoring two poles in the ground.
3. Attach a crossbar pole to your main supports at about shoulder level, securing both ends with rope.
4. Gather long branches or poles and lean them against the crossbar. Be sure to angle them out

far enough so that you will be able to sit comfortably underneath the shelter. Block the ends of your lean-to with additional branches; if necessary, tie the end branches in place with rope. Fit the branches as closely together as possible to keep the wind out.

5. Collect lots of small boughs and sticks and, starting at the bottom, layer them like shingles against the lean-to. Moss, pine needles, and lichen-covered branches work well, too. This will help insulate your fort and keep you warm as well as sheltered from the wind. If you have a tarp or canvas, you can secure it on top to water-proof your lean-to.

101

Mini Meatloaves pack a punch in your lunch! Eat as is or sandwich between two thick slabs of bread. Substitute ground turkey for beef for a lean and mean alternative. Cold sesame noodles make a great alternative to a sandwich, and PB & J Bars provide quick energy. Make lots of fruit chews and always have handy to throw into your lunch bag.

MINI MEATLOAVES

1 1/2 pounds ground beef
1 cup soft bread crumbs
1/4 cup chopped onions
1 teaspoon dried Italian seasoning
1/4 cup ketchup
1 1/2 cups zucchini, shredded
1 egg, slightly beaten
1/2 teaspoon salt
Muffin pan

1. Heat oven to 400° F.
2. In large bowl, combine all ingredients except ketchup, mixing thoroughly.
3. Spoon approximately 1/3 cup beef mixture into each of the 12 medium muffin cups. Press lightly. Spread ketchup generously over each one.
4. Bake for 20 minutes or until centers are no longer pink.
5. Remove meatloaves from pan. Let cool.
6. Freeze meatloaves and defrost as needed.
7. Pack in tupperware container with a whole-wheat bread roll and ketchup packets for a hearty lunch.

Makes 12 loaves.

FUN FRUIT CHEWS

3 cups juice (orange, pineapple, grape, mango, etc.)
five (7-gram) gelatin packets

1. In a small mixing bowl, stir gelatin into 1 cup of fruit juice. Set aside.
2. In a small saucepan, bring 1 cup of juice to a boil. Add gelatin-juice mix and stir. Stir in remaining cup of juice.
3. Remove from heat and pour into an 8-inch casserole dish. Refrigerate until firm.
4. Cut into fun shapes and wrap individually.

Makes 18 to 24 chews. Chews will keep in the refrigerator for about a week.

BROWN BAG BONANZA

COLD SESAME NOODLES

8 ounces soba (lo mein) noodles or other thin pasta cooked
6 tablespoons peanut butter or tahini
$^1/_4$ cup hot water
2 tablespoons sesame oil
$^1/_4$ cup soy sauce
$^1/_2$ teaspoon ground ginger
1 clove garlic, minced
2–3 tablespoons green onions or chives, minced
$^1/_2$ cup bean sprouts

1. In a small bowl, whisk peanut butter or tahini, hot water, sesame oil, soy sauce, ginger, and garlic together until they form a smooth paste.
2. In a large bowl, toss noodles with peanut-butter paste, green onions, and bean sprouts.
3. Refrigerate. Pack in a thermos for lunch and eat with chopsticks.

Makes 4 servings.

PB & J BARS

2 cups uncooked oats
$^1/_3$ cup peanut-butter
$^1/_2$ cup grape jelly

1. Preheat oven to 350°F.
2. In medium bowl, combine all ingredients and mix thoroughly.
3. Spread mixture into greased 8-inch-square pan.
4. Bake for 25 minutes. Let cool.
5. Cut into bars and wrap individually for lunches.

Makes 8 bars.

104

SUPER LUNCH-SACK STUFFERS

- Pickles
- Graham crackers "sand-wiched" with chocolate-marshmallow spread
- Pretzels
- Bananas
- Apples
- Grapes
- Peeled orange

- Baby carrots
- Cherry tomatoes
- Yogurt cups
- Pudding cups
- Apple sauce
- Juice boxes
- Crackers with sliced cheese and salami
- Fortune cookies

- Popcorn
- String cheese
- Hard-boiled eggs
- Fig bars
- Edamame
- Sunflower seeds
- Peanuts in their shells
- Homemade cookies or brownies

BETTER BROWN BAG TIPS:

- Put juice boxes or water bottles in freezer the night before. You'll have a cold drink for lunch and an ice pack to keep the rest of your lunch cool.
- Keep lettuce, tomatoes, and other "moist" foods wrapped separately. Build your sandwich at lunchtime and avoid soggy sammies!
- Pack travel-sized moist hand wipes for easy cleanup after you eat.

- Thermoses can be for more than just juice. You can keep last night's left-over spaghetti, chili, or soup warm for several hours. Or, keep pasta salads, potato salad, or fruit salads nice and cool.
- Save prepackaged condiments from your favorite take-out restaurants for extra bread-spreads or dipping sauces.

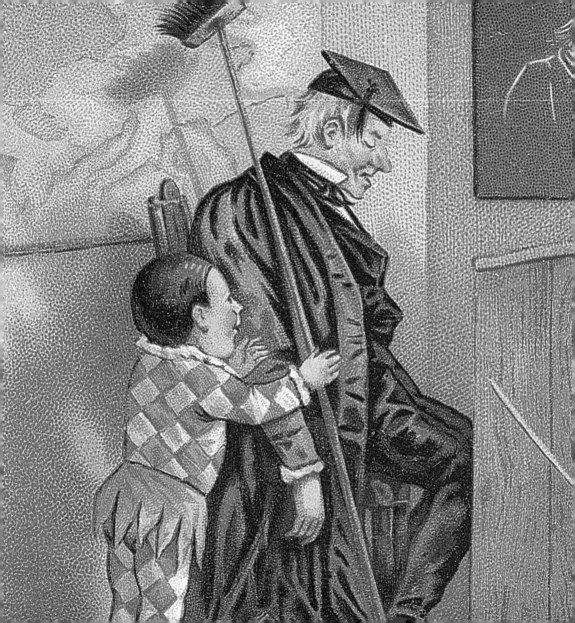

Young Athletes

BASEBALL

On July 22, 1887, FREDERICK JOSEPH CHAPMAN (1872–1957) was 14 years, 239 days old when he pitched for Philadelphia in the American Association, becoming the youngest player in professional baseball history. He did not play again, however.

BASKETBALL

When JERMAINE O'NEAL (b. 1978) made his professional basketball debut with the Portland Trailblazers on December 5, 1996, he became the youngest-ever NBA player, at 18 years, 53 days of age.

EXPLORING

At the age of 10, ROBERT SCHUMANN (b. 1982), of the UK, and his father decided to go vacationing at the North Pole. Arriving there by plane on April 6, 1992, Schumann became the youngest explorer ever to arrive at the northernmost point of the planet. On December 29, 1993, at age 11, he reached the South Pole by mountain bike, having flown to within a short distance of his destination.

HIKING

MICHAEL COGSWELL was 6 years old when he finished hiking the length of the approximately 2,160-mile-long (3,476-km) Appalachian Trail with his mother and stepfather in 1980. It took them eight and a half months to finish the world's longest designated footpath, which stretches from Katahdin, Maine, to Springer Mountain, Georgia.

MOUNTAIN CLIMBING

Although his age at the time is still somewhat in dispute, Nepal's SHAMBU TAMANG (b. 1955) became the youngest person ever to ascend 29,035-foot-high (8,850-meter) Mt. Everest, on May 5, 1973. He's thought to have been 17 years, 6 months, and 15 days old when he reached the summit.

OLYMPICS

ROBERT BRUCE MATTHIAS (b. 1930) became the youngest male Olympic champion when he won the decathlon, held August 5–6 in the 1948 Olympic Games, in London. He was 17 years, 263 days old.

SOCCER

EDSON ARANTES DO NASCIMENTO (b. 1940), better known as Pelé, distinguished himself as the youngest scorer in a World Cup final match when he scored for Brazil against Wales in Gothenburg, Sweden, on June 19, 1958. At 17 years, 239 days old, he was hailed as a Brazilian hero. They nicknamed him the *Perola Negra* ("Black Pearl").

TENNIS

In 1985, BORIS BECKER (b. 1967), of West Germany, became the youngest Wimbledon champion when he won the tournament at the age of 17 years, 227 days.

109

GET SPORTY!

Tees, baskets, field goals, and nets! How many ways can you win a set? Brush up on your knowledge of some of our favorite pastimes.

BASEBALL

Nobody can really be sure when baseball began in America, but some say the game started in Cooperstown, New York (home of the National Baseball Hall of Fame and Museum), in 1839. It was first played professionally in 1869, and since then the sport has grown to thirty teams in two leagues (the American and National Leagues). The regular baseball season stretches from April through September, with the two best teams (one from each league) making it to the World Series in October. The World Series is a best-of-seven showdown, alternating between the two teams' hometowns, that determines who takes home the title of champion.

TENNIS

Tennis was first played in France as early as the twelfth century, when players knocked a ball around a walled-in court with the palms of their hands. The game gradually developed the use of paddles and then racquets to hit a ball over a net. These days it's played with high-tech racquets on one of three surfaces: clay, grass, or cement. Unlike team sports, tennis has no "season," but goes year round, all over the world. There are countless tournaments and events for players to establish their rankings, but as for Grand Slams, there are only four: the Australian Open in Melbourne (January), the French Open, near Paris (May), Wimbledon, in London, England (July), and the U.S. Open in New York City (September). The game itself has a very unusual scoring system: players score points to win games; to win a set, a player must win at least six games and lead his or her opponent by two games. The player who wins the most sets (usually two out of three) wins the match!

BASKETBALL

Basketball is, without a doubt, the zoomingest game on television. From start to finish, the players zigzag across the court, leaping to make baskets and whipping the ball through the air.

The game was invented in 1891 by a Massachusetts gym teacher, Dr. James Naismith. Basketball moves almost without stopping and it is made up of four periods, each 12 minutes long. The twenty-nine teams in the National Basketball Association (NBA) play from October to June, with the best teams from the Eastern and Western Conferences going head to head in a best-of-seven play-off at the end.

FOOTBALL

American football's origins can be found in the rough British sport of rugby, which was brought over to the United States in the mid-1800s. The boys at Harvard College changed some rules (including the use of a new egg-shaped ball) and called it "football," but it wasn't until 1880 that a student at Yale came up with the rules for modern football. The rules have continued to change over the years, as have the setup of leagues, conferences, and so forth. Currently there is only one league—the National Football League (NFL)—divided into the American and National Football Conferences. The cream of these crops play each other in the hyped-up extravaganza known as the Super Bowl—one game, held in January. The regular season lasts from September to early January, with the thirty-two teams playing just one game per week. If you've ever watched a football game and seen how brutal it can be, you can understand why!

GOLF

Golf began in fourteenth-century (1300s) Scotland, where the rolling green hills, grazed clean by sheep, were ideal for knocking a little ball around. This very landscape is the model for modern golf courses around the world, set in deserts, along coasts, and among forests. Because it's spread out all over the planet, golf is in swing

year round, with the best players coming out to compete on courses that are both challenging and beautiful. One tournament, the Pebble Beach Pro-Am (which stands for "Professional-Amateur"), held in southern California, attracts Hollywood stars who play alongside the pros. Some, like comedians Bill Murray and Ray Romano, have turned the tournament into more than just a sporting event with their goofy antics on the course.

SOCCER

The early history of modern soccer resembles the history of the British Empire. Before the codification of official Football Association laws (which made no mention of the allowable number of players or the duration of play), soccer games were disorganized conflicts with fields as large as towns, and as many as 500 participants involved in a brutal daylong conflict. During the late nineteenth century, however, Britain began taking the game to various parts of the world, along with the two other English favorites, cricket and rugby.

Of the three, soccer has become the most popular international sport. By the second Olympic Games, which were held in Paris in 1900, soccer had already been introduced as a demonstration game. Eight years later, England defeated Denmark in the first official Olympic soccer final during the 1908 London Games. The world governing body for soccer, Fédération Internationale de Football Association (FIFA), held its first meeting in 1904 in Paris. It was attended by seven member nations. Today, the fact that FIFA's international membership has swelled to over 150 national associations—rivaled only by the International Olympic Committee—gives testament to soccer's enduring legacy.

VOLLEYBALL

Most volleyball enthusiasts will place the birthplace of beach volleyball in Santa Monica, California, some time in the early 1920s. Families played in teams of six on courts set up on the beach. The first two-man beach volleyball game was also played in Santa Monica in 1930, and in 1947, the first official two-man beach tournament was held at State Beach, California. In fact, the sport can trace most of its major developments in the Golden State, but its Santa Monica heritage didn't keep it from attaining international scope. At the 1996 Atlanta Olympic Games, with twenty-four men's teams and sixteen women's teams representing their countries, beach volleyball became an official tournament event.

ICE HOCKEY

Ice hockey began about 200 years ago when schoolboys in Windsor, Nova Scotia, Canada, took the Irish game of hurling, changed the rules around, and played it on the ice of a favorite local skating pond. Since 1904, when a league was formed in the United States, ice hockey has been a professional sport, with thirty teams competing across the States and Canada. The regular season starts up in October and lasts all winter long. It winds down in April, but playoffs among the best teams extend through May. The Stanley Cup Playoffs, ice hockey's final series, are held in June.

MUHAMMAD ALI (b. 1942) first achieved fame when he won a gold medal in boxing at the 1960 Olympics. Later, he became the first man to win the heavyweight title three times. Ali was fast and graceful, and outside of the boxing ring, "The Greatest" was known for his witty rhymes and poetry. More than that, though, Ali was both appreciated and scorned for his anti-war beliefs, standing up for his Islamic religion, and his willingness to have boxing matches in faraway places to make people aware of other countries and cultures.

JIM BROWN (b. 1936) is one of football's great legends. A fullback for the Cleveland Browns from 1957 to 1966, Brown was known for his power and speed. He scored 126 touchdowns, 106 of them by rushing. He led the NFL in rushing for eight of the nine years he played. Brown retired at 30, to become an actor and start an organization to help young people.

HEROES OF SPORTS

WAYNE GRETZKY (b. 1961) began skating on the frozen river near his grandparents' farm when he was only 2. Like many kids in Canada, he grew up watching and playing hockey during much of his free time. Gretzky is considered the most influential professional hockey player of all time, and when he retired in 1999, he held sixty-one National Hockey League records.

MICHAEL JORDAN (b. 1963) is probably the greatest basketball player ever to play the game. Before becoming a pro, Michael attended the University of North Carolina and was twice voted College Player of the Year. While in school, he also helped the U.S. win a gold medal in basketball at the 1984 Olympics. Jordan went on to become a superstar for the Chicago Bulls and has helped them win six national championships. He has been awarded the Most Valuable Player trophy five times.

BABE RUTH (1895–1948) was so difficult as a child that his parents sent him to a home run by Catholic brothers when he was 7. It was there that he learned to play baseball. He learned so well that he was famous citywide by 19, and signed up by the Orioles. Later, he went to the Boston Red Sox to play, and finally to the New York Yankees. This bigger-than-life national hero played a total of twenty full seasons, leading the league in home runs twelve times, in runs eight times, in RBIs six times, and in slugging thirteen times.

TIGER WOODS (b. 1975) is one of golf's all-time most successful players. When he was only 2, he was on TV putting with the comedian Bob Hope. At 3, he scored an unbelievable 48 on nine holes. At 15, he was the youngest ever to win the U.S. Junior Amateur; at 18, the youngest ever to win the U.S. Amateur; and at 21, the youngest Masters Golf Tournament champion. Tiger has won forty-two tournaments, and became the first person ever to hold all four professional major championships at the same time.

Play Ball

by Shel Silverstein

Okay, let's play, I think that we
Have everyone we need.
I'll be the strong-armed pitcher
Who can throw with blinding speed.
And Pete will be the catcher
Who squats low and pounds his mitt,
And Mike will be the home-run king
Who snarls and waits to hit
One, loud and long and hard and high,
Way out beyond the wall.
So let's get start— What? *You?* Oh, yes,
You can be the ball!

Score!

Next time you want to play a fast and furious game of air hockey, skip the arcade and go for something with a bit of magnetic appeal. With a few basic materials and some creativity, you can make a hockey arena that's sure to be full of action and excitement. Then you can host your own Winter Olympics any time of the year. So grab an opponent and face off!

Extra-large shoebox lid, ruler, colored markers, four paper cups, 3 x 5 index card, scissors, masking tape, rubber bands, 2 bar magnets, 2 chopsticks, 2 metallic washers, red and blue nail polish or paint, plastic button

1. To make your hockey arena, turn the shoebox lid upside down. Draw a straight line across the middle of the lid to create the center court line. Place a paper cup in the middle of the lid and trace the circle to complete the court design.
2. For the goal nets, fold the index card in half lengthwise and cut along the crease. Fold back a $1^{1}/_{4}$-inch flap on each end of both halves of the index card. Tape flaps to the shoebox lid.
3. Raise the playing field by taping an upside-down paper cup to each corner of the shoebox lid.
4. Use rubber bands to secure a magnet to the end of each chopstick.
5. Paint each washer a different color (red or blue) to identify each team.

TO PLAY: Use the button as a hockey puck and place it in the middle of the court. Place the red and blue washers on either side of the puck. The players hold their chopstick magnets under the shoebox lid to make his washer move on the court. Each player tries to make his washer hit the puck into the goal for one point. The player with the most points after ten minutes wins.

What lies at the bottom of the ocean and twitches?

A nervous wreck.

When do ghosts usually appear?

Just before someone screams.

What is the difference between a jeweller and a jailer?

One sells watches and the other watches cells.

What do you call a chicken at the North Pole?

Lost.

THAT'S FUNNY!

Why do dragons sleep during the day?
So they can fight knights.

What is black and white, black and white, black and white?
A penguin caught in a revolving door.

What do you get when you cross a shark with a parrot?
An animal that talks your head off.

How do you say good-bye to a vampire?
Immediately.

Why did the mayonnaise blush?
It saw the salad dressing!

What should you do if a wild elephant charges you in the jungle?
Pay him, dummy!

123

Passing the Willy Wonka Chocolate factory each day on his walk to school is absolute torture for Charlie Bucket. Wafting scents of rich, delicious chocolate makes his hollow stomach ache. So when the factory announces its five golden ticket contest, Charlie doesn't dare dream that he might be among the lucky winners of a private factory tour conducted by the eccentric Mr. Wonka himself! The first four to find golden tickets hidden in Wonka confections are greedy Augustus Gloop, spoiled Veruca Salt, gum-snapping Violet Beauregarde, and television-obsessed Mike Teavee—not a worthy winner in the bunch. When our kind-hearted hero, Charlie, finds a dollar in the snow, he races to buy just one candy bar. No ticket. He buys another, and—the last golden ticket! Roald Dahl (1916-1990) was born in Wales . He spent his childhood in London, and at the age of 26 moved to America to write—first short stories and adult fiction, then, by 1960 he began to write children's books for which he is best known. His trademark was always his complete disregard for the opinions of grown-ups. Dahl was posthumously honored with the Millennium Children's Book Award in 2000 for Charlie and the Chocolate Factory (1964).

Mr. Wonka turned right.

He turned left.

He turned right again.

The passages were sloping steeper and steeper downhill now.

Then suddenly, Mr. Wonka stopped. In front of him, there was a shiny metal door. The party crowded round. On the door, in large letters, it said:

THE CHOCOLATE ROOM

"An important room, this!" cried Mr. Wonka, taking a bunch of keys from his pocket and slipping one into the keyhole of the door. "This is the nerve center of the whole factory, the heart of the whole business! And so beautiful! I insist upon my rooms being beautiful! I can't abide ugliness in factories! In we go, then! But do be careful, my dear children! Don't lose your heads! Don't get overexcited! Keep very calm!"

Mr. Wonka opened the door. Five children and nine grownups pushed their ways in—and *oh*, what an amazing sight it was that now met their eyes!

They were looking down upon a lovely valley.

Charlie and The Chocolate Factory

by Roald Dahl

There were green meadows on either side of the valley, and along the bottom of it there flowed a great brown river.

What is more, there was a tremendous waterfall halfway along the river—a steep cliff over which the water curled and rolled in a solid sheet, and then went crashing down into a boiling churning whirlpool of froth and spray.

Below the waterfall (and this was the most astonishing sight of all), a whole mass of enormous glass pipes were dangling down into the river from somewhere high up in the ceiling! They really were enormous, those pipes. There must have been a dozen of them at least, and they were sucking up the brownish muddy water from the river and carrying it away to goodness knows where. And because they were made of glass, you could see the liquid flowing and bubbling along inside them, and above the noise of the waterfall, you could hear the never-ending suck-suck-sucking sound of the pipes as they did their work.

Graceful trees and bushes were growing along the riverbanks—weeping willows and alders and tall clumps of rhododendrons with their pink and red and mauve blossoms. In the meadows there were thousands of buttercups.

"There!" cried Mr. Wonka, dancing up and down and pointing his gold-topped cane at the great brown river. "It's all chocolate! Every drop of that river is hot melted chocolate of the finest quality. The *very* finest quality. There's enough chocolate in there to fill *every* bathtub in the *entire* country! *And* all the swimming pools as well!

"It's all chocolate! Every drop of that river is hot melted chocolate of the finest quality."

Isn't it *terrific*? And just look at my pipes! They suck up the chocolate and carry it away to all the other rooms in the factory where it is needed! Thousands of gallons an hour, my dear children! Thousands and thousands of gallons!"

The children and their parents were too flabbergasted to speak. They were staggered. They were dumfounded. They were bewildered and dazzled. They were completely bowled over by the hugeness of the whole thing. They simply stood and stared.

"The waterfall is *most* important!" Mr. Wonka went on. "It mixes the chocolate! It churns it up! It pounds it and beats it! It makes it light and frothy! No other factory in the world mixes its chocolate by waterfall! But it's the *only* way to do it properly! The *only* way! And do you like my trees?" he cried, pointing with his stick. "And my lovely bushes? Don't you think they look pretty? I told you I hated ugliness! And of course they are *all* eatable! All made of something different and delicious! And do you like my meadows? Do you like my grass and my buttercups? The grass you are standing on, my dear little ones, is made of a new kind of soft, minty sugar that I've just invented! I call it swudge! Try a blade! Please do! It's delectable!"

Automatically, everybody bent down and picked one blade of grass—everybody,

Violet Beauregarde, before tasting her blade of grass, took the piece of world-record-breaking chewing gum out of her mouth and stuck it carefully behind her ear.

that is, except Augustus Gloop, who took a big handful.

And Violet Beauregarde, before tasting her blade of grass, took the piece of world-record-breaking chewing gum out of her mouth and stuck it carefully behind her ear.

"Isn't it *wonderful!*" whispered Charlie. "Hasn't it got a wonderful taste, Grandpa?"

"I could eat the whole field!" said Grandpa Joe, grinning with delight. "I could go around on all fours like a cow and eat every blade of grass in the field!"

"Try a buttercup!" cried Mr. Wonka. "They're even *nicer!*"

Sweet Feats

LARGEST MILKSHAKE

Manhattan's Ira Freehof, who has the unique distinction of owning the celebrated Comfort Diners, also broke the record for world's largest milkshake on August 1, 2000, with a 6,000-gallon classic Black & White shake that shattered the previous record of 4,603.24 gallons.

LARGEST LOLLIPOP

Jolly Rancher presented the world's largest lollipop when it unwrapped its giant-sized replica of its regular cherry lollipop on June 25, 2002. At an exceptionally large 4,016 pounds and measuring over 5 feet square and 18.9 inches thick, the giant sucker broke the old record by more than 1,000 pounds.

LARGEST CHOCOLATE MODEL

The largest chocolate model ever built weighed 8,818 pounds, 6 ounces, and was in the shape of a traditional Spanish sailing ship. Put into commission in February 1991 by the Gremi Provincial de Pastisseria, Confiteria i Bolleria school in Barcelona, the chocolate vessel measured 42 feet, 8 inches by 27 feet, 10 1/2 inches by 8 feet, 2 1/2 inches.

LARGEST BUBBLE-GUM BUBBLE

Measured under the strict rules of the fiercely competitive activity of bubble-gum bubble blowing, the largest diameter for a bubble was 23 inches, by Susan Montgomery Williams of Fresno, CA, on July 19, 1994.

TALLEST CAKE

The tallest cake ever created measured a whopping 101 feet, 2 1/2 inches high. Made by Beth Cornell Trevorrow with a team of helpers at the Shiawassee County Fairgrounds, MI, it had one hundred tiers, the last of which was finished on August 5, 1990.

You won't be able to resist these scrumptious Snickerdoodles or Norm's Master Brownies served hot out of the oven with a scoop of vanilla ice cream. Monster cookies are great for monster appetites. And the next time you're planning to go on a long bike ride or a hike in the woods, be sure to take some Hike & Bike bars along. They're perfect grab-and-go energy boosters and perfectly delicious! Throw some fudge in your pack also, you deserve a treat!

SNICKERDOODLES

1 cup butter, softened to room temperature
1 1/2 cups sugar
2 eggs, room temperature
1 teaspoon vanilla
2 3/4 cups flour
2 teaspoons cream of tartar
1 teaspoon baking powder
2 tablespoons sugar
2 tablespoons cinnamon

1. Cream butter, 1 1/2 cups sugar, eggs, and vanilla.
2. Sift flour, cream of tartar, and baking soda together and stir into creamed mixture. Chill dough in refrigerator for 1 hour.
3. Preheat oven to 400°F.
4. Roll dough into walnut-size balls. Combine remaining sugar and cinnamon in a shallow dish. Roll dough balls in mixture until well coated.
5. Place cookies about 2 inches apart on ungreased cookie sheet. Bake 8–10 minutes until lightly brown, but still soft.

Makes about 4 dozen cookies.

MARSHMALLOW NUT FUDGE

2 sticks (1 cup) butter, softened
16 ounces marshmallow creme
2 teaspoons vanilla
18 ounces (1 1/2 packages) semisweet chocolate chips
2 cups walnuts, chopped
4 cups sugar
12 ounces evaporated milk

1. In a large bowl, mix butter, marshmallow creme, and vanilla. Fold in chocolate chips and walnuts.
2. In a large (6- to 8-quart) saucepan, combine sugar and milk. Bring to boil and cook for

exactly 9 minutes, stirring constantly. Remove from heat. (*CAUTION: Do not leave unattended. If mixture begins to boil over, turn down heat.*)

3. Combine with butter mixture and mix thoroughly.
4. Pour into a greased 13- by 9-inch pan and refrigerate for at least 3 hours. (Can be stored in the freezer.) Cut into bite-size pieces.

Makes 24 to 30 pieces.

MONSTER COOKIES

1 pound butter, softened to room temperature
4 cups white sugar
2 pounds brown sugar
1 tablespoon vanilla
1 tablespoon light corn syrup
8 teaspoons baking soda
3 pounds chunky peanut butter
12 eggs
18 cups oatmeal (42-ounce box)
1 pound M&M's candies
1 pound chocolate chips

1. Preheat oven to 350°F.
2. In a large bowl, cream butter, white sugar, brown sugar, vanilla, corn syrup, and baking soda. Stir in peanut butter. Beat in eggs, two at a time.
3. Mix in oatmeal, M&M's, and chocolate chips until well blended.
4. Use an ice-cream scoop to drop balls of dough onto an ungreased cookie sheet about 2 inches apart. Bake for 12 minutes.

Makes 6 to 10 dozen cookies.

NORM'S MASTER BROWNIES

1¹/2 sticks (³/4 cup) butter, softened to room temperature
12 ounces chocolate chips or sweetened baking chocolate
3 eggs, at room temperature
1 cup sugar
2 teaspoons vanilla
pinch baking powder
1 cup flour

1. Preheat oven to 350°F.
2. Melt butter and chocolate in a saucepan over low heat, stirring often. Remove from heat when melted and let stand at room temperature for about 10 minutes.

OR: Melt butter and chocolate in microwave on medium high in 1-minute intervals, stirring in between timings.

3. In a mixing bowl, beat eggs, sugar, vanilla, and baking powder until fluffy. Stir in chocolate mixture. Gradually add flour, stirring with a fork until just blended.

4. Pour batter into a greased 13- by 9-inch pan. Bake for 20 to 25 minutes, or until tester comes out clean. Remove from oven and let cool before cutting into squares.

Makes 18 to 24 brownies.

HIKE & BIKE BARS

2 sticks (1 cup) butter
1 1/2 cups brown sugar
2 teaspoons vanilla extract
2 large eggs
2 1/2 cups flour
1 1/2 teaspoons baking powder
1/2 teaspoon salt
1/2 cup peanut butter
1/2 cup walnuts, chopped
1/2 cup white chocolate chips
1/2 cup chocolate chips
1/2 cup dried cranberries
1/2 cup golden raisins

1. Preheat oven to 350°F.

2. In a large bowl, beat butter, sugar, and vanilla extract until creamy. Beat in eggs, one at a time.

3. Gradually beat in flour, baking powder, and salt until blended.

4. Fold in peanut butter. Fold in nuts, chips, and dried fruit until combined.

5. Spread cookie dough mixture evenly into a greased 13- by 9-inch pan. Bake for 23 to 28 minutes, or until golden brown on top and center feels firm. Cool to room temperature before cutting into bars. Bars can be wrapped in wax paper and stored in airtight containers at room temperature up to two weeks.

Makes 18 to 24 bars.

More Twisters!

Try to say each of the following twisters five times as fast as you can!

Three free throws. Three free throws. Three free throw

Six sharp smart sharks. Six sharp smart sharks. Six sharp smar

Six selfish shellfis

Sixty-six sickly chicks. Sixty-six sickly chicks. Sixty-si

ree free throws. Three free throws.

arks. Six sharp smart sharks. Six sharp smart sharks.

Toy boat. Toy boat. Toy boat. Toy boat. Toy boat.

Six selfish shellfish.

x selfish shellfish. Six selfish shellfish. Six selfish shellfish.

ckly chicks. Sixty-six sickly chicks. Sixty-six sickly chicks.

Well, if you want to sing out, sing out.
And if you want to be free, be free.
'Cause there's a million things to be.
You know that there are.
And if you want to live high, live high.
And if you want to live low, live low.
'Cause there's a million ways to go.
You know that there are.

You can do what you want.
The opportunity's on.
And if you find a new way,
You can do it today.
You can make it all true.
And you can make it undo, you see.
Ah, it's easy.
Ah, you only need to know.

Well, if you want to say yes, say yes.
And if you want to say no, say no.
'Cause there's a million ways to go.
You know that there are.
And if you want to be me, be me.
And if you want to be you, be you.
'Cause there's a million things to do.
You know that there are.

Well, if you want to sing out, sing out.
And if you want to be free, be free.
'Cause there's a million things to be.
You know that there are,
You know that there are,
You know that there are
You know that there are.

FREDERICK DOUGLASS (1817–95), the son of a black slave woman and a white man, escaped slavery himself when he was twenty-one. One day he was asked to speak in front of a group of abolitionists, or people against slavery, about his experiences. From that time on, he would continue to give speeches and write articles and books about equal rights among people of all colors. He advised Abraham Lincoln and even recruited black soldiers for the North's Union Army during the Civil War. He is considered by many to be the founder of the American Civil Rights movement.

MOHANDAS "MAHATMA" K. GANDHI (1869–1948) was born in India, but his parents sent him to England to study law. He then moved to South Africa, where he became a champion of the rights of Indian immigrants who were mistreated by local society. It was there that Gandhi first came up with the idea of using passive resistance instead of violence against injustices. When he returned to India, he led the Indian National Congress and took up the struggle of achieving independence from Britain, which ruled over the country. Ultimately, Gandhi and his nonviolent ways triumphed for India's freedom. Many years later, his name is still an international symbol of progress achieved through peaceful methods.

MARTIN LUTHER KING, JR. (1929–68) was a minister in Montgomery, Alabama, in 1955 when a black woman, Rosa Parks, took a stand against unfair rules by refusing to sit in the back of the bus just because of her color. Right after that, King led a boycott of city buses, which resulted in black people being able to legally sit anywhere they wanted. King later headed up peaceful demonstrations against racism that generated lots of attention—enough attention to cause the creation of the Civil Rights Act to protect people no matter their color. In 1963, he led a Civil Rights march on Washington, D.C., that brought together more than 200,000 people. The refrain of his most famous speech, about his

HEROES OF PEACE

hopes for racial harmony, was "I have a dream." In 1964, King was awarded the Nobel Peace Prize.

NELSON MANDELA (b. 1918) was one of the leading figures of a political organization called the African National Congress. He studied law and was actively opposed to apartheid, which was a policy that gave black people lesser rights than whites in South Africa. From 1964 to 1990, Mandela was kept in jail for opposing the government and its unjust laws; instead of disappearing, however, he became a symbol all over the world for resisting racism. In 1993, Mandela and the president who released him shared the Nobel Peace Prize. A year later, Nelson Mandela was elected the first black president of South Africa.

Take from the rich to give to the poor! That is the code by which Robin Hood and his band of merry men live. The outlaws of Sherwood Forest—discovering that the king's laws are often flawed and that the king's men are nearly all unjust—create their own set of rules. Their many "good" deeds are all done in the name of the common folk. Their adventures serve to aid the poor and oppressed, while often having the comic side effect of frustrating the rich and powerful. Ann McGovern's *Robin Hood* (1991) is an adaptation of a centuries-old classic. Whether or not Robin Hood was a real man remains unknown. Many ballads circulated around England about the hero of the people. The first appearance of Robin Hood's name in print was probably in *Piers Plowman* (c. 1378), by William Langland, in which a drunken priest cannot repeat the Lord's Prayer but knows the "rhymes of Robin Hood."

t was a merry May morning, and Robin Hood walked with a bold heart and steps as brisk as the winds that blew through Sherwood Forest. For he was on his way to Nottingham Town, where he would test his skill alongside the Sheriff's best bowmen at Nottingham Fair.

Though this brave, stalwart youth was only seventeen, as an archer he had no peer in all of England. So Robin's hopes of winning the Sheriff's prize of a purse of gold were higher than the floating clouds in the bright May morning sky.

Strolling along, he thought of nothing but the coming contest—and of fair Marian, the young maid to whom Robin had given his heart and his pledge. He thought of how her black eyes would gleam when he handed her the prize.

Now he whistled; now he sang; now he leaped across the brook, taking care that his stout bow and score of arrows would not tumble as he ran free as the King's deer in the forest.

Then, as Robin came out of the sun-dappled woods into a mossy clearing, he came across a band of seven foresters, making merry with food and drink beneath a great tree.

Their leader wiped a bit of meat from his lips and called out to Robin, "Halloa,

Robin Hood of Sherwood Forest

by Ann McGovern

143

young chuck. Why art thou out among the woods when thou shouldst be home on thy mother's lap?"

The others laughed heartily, but Robin's blood ran hot, for he felt himself as much a man as any of them there.

"Mark well where I am going," Robin said sharply. "I'm off to the Fair to try my bow against such bold and ill-mannered knaves as thou."

"Hold thy tongue, sprite," said the head forester, who did not take kindly to Robin's sharp reply. "Try arms with us now, if thou art so certain of thy skill. A purseful of silver pennies is thine if those toy arrows should hit their mark."

"Enough said," replied Robin. "Only choose thy target."

The forester's grin was wicked. "Aye, but thou hast heeded not the rest of the wager. If thou hit not the mark, I'll baste thy head on both sides."

"The wager is made," cried Robin. "My head against the silver pennies."

The forester pointed to a crest in the wood, five-score yards distant, where a herd of gentle deer were grazing.

"Then pick me down the leader," said the forester.

Aghast, Robin cried, "Ye know these are the King's deer—that it is death to the man who kills one!"

"Thou are afraid then?" said the forester, notching an arrow.

> "Try arms with us now, if thou art so certain of thy skill. A purseful of silver pennies is thine if those toy arrows should hit their mark."

> ## "Thy head will hang for having killed one of the King's deer."

Robin's answer was to bend his bow.

A twang of the bowstring, a humming of the goose feather—and the next moment the leader of the herd leaped high, then fell, and straightway blood appeared on its tawny coat.

Robin turned to the forester, triumph on his face.

"Ho!" cried the forester. "Now thou hast done it, my sorry lad. Thy head will hang for having killed one of the King's deer."

"But 'twas thou that challenged me," cried Robin, his face flushing red as the blood on the fallen deer.

"But 'twas *thou* that let fly the arrow," said the chief forester. "Men, seize this rascal!"

"I wager the Sheriff will be pleased to see such a pretty outlaw," another forester cried.

Thereupon Robin, who had been edging closer to the thicket, turned and dashed into the wood.

Deep into the greenwood he ran, when of a sudden an arrow whizzed so close to him it drew blood from his ear. Another arrow and still another flew, but fortunately for Robin, all fell wide of their mark.

And still he ran until the angry growls of the foresters were swallowed by the trees of Sherwood Forest.

Robin sat down, his back against a strong oak tree; he was overwhelmed by bitter-sad thoughts.

"Am I doomed, then, to the life of an outlaw, forever hiding in the greenwood? And all because I killed a creature in the forest of the King—the forest that by rights belongs to the people? Aye, it is the foresters themselves who should be in my place this moment, and I should be on my merry way to the Fair."

Robin sank deeper into gloom as he thought of all those whom he would see no more—his cousins, his friends, and his dear love, Maid Marian, who now surely would never be allowed to see him again.

> "Fortunes such as mine that fall so low can only rise again," he said to himself.

But Robin was made of hearty stuff, and his gloom soon lifted. "Fortunes such as mine that fall so low can only rise again," he said to himself.

Whereupon he chuckled. "So long as I am an outlaw, methinks I should be a worthy one. Two hundred pounds would be a fair price to set upon this lucky head," he said, stroking the place where the forester's arrow had almost put an end to him.

Of a sudden, a rustle in the thicket caused Robin to stiffen. He leaped to his feet, his bow in readiness.

Out of the woods stepped two men. At the sight of them Robin gave a glad cry, for he knew them well.

One was Midge the Miller's son, the other was Will Stutely; and each had a tale to tell of why he now called Sherwood forest his home.

As Robin listened, his eyes hardened and anger rose within him. For as the men told their stories, he came to realize what path his fortunes must take him.

Life in those olden days was oftentimes cruel and unjust for the good and the poor folk, who were forced to pay large sums of money to the nobles and the rich. High taxes, outrageous rents, and fines made the poor even poorer, as they tried to scratch a life out of the fields and forests.

Indeed, the laws of the rich were such that, whosoever stepped into the King's forest either to kill a deer to keep his family from starving, or to cut wood to keep them from freezing, was guilty of crime; and, if caught, he could be hanged.

That to the evil-hearted Sheriff of Nottingham they would give no mercy.

So it was that men, such as Robin Hood, Will Stutely, Midge the Miller's son, and others as honest as these were now outlaws, though truly it was the unjust laws that had made them so.

In Sherwood Forest they came to dwell, deep in the greenwood where none could find them. There they were safe, for a time, from the noose of the Sheriff's hangman.

Before the year was out, a company of five-score brave and stalwart outlawed yeomen came to Sherwood Forest and chose Robin Hood as their leader.

And as all men live better by rules, so did they make strict ones so that they might help the wronged and at the same time punish the wrong-doers.

Each man who wore the Lincoln green of Robin Hood's band willingly took these vows:

- That they would harm no innocent man working with his plow or walking in the greenwood.

- That knights and squires of good heart would be unharmed, as well as any child or woman, or any man in women's company.
- That to these they would give help, and would fight to give back that which had been cruelly taken away.
- That they would bring woe to those fat abbots and cruel nobles, and all who were unjust to the poor.
- That from these they would take all their ill-gotten gains.
- That if any man lied or said he had no money when his purse was filled with silver or gold—from this man would they help themselves generously.
- That to the evil-hearted Sheriff of Nottingham they would give no mercy.

And each man who swelled the ranks of Robin's band was true to the vows he took.

After a while much good was spoken of the outlaws by the gentle folk to whom Robin brought food, safety, or help in times of danger.

But the greedy rich and those without mercy kept a watchful eye, for they much feared Robin and his merry men in Sherwood Forest.

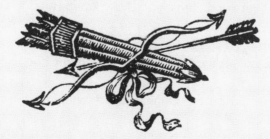

If I Had A Hammer

by Lee Hays and Pete Seeger

If I had a hammer I'd hammer in the morning,
I'd hammer in the evening all over this land
I'd hammer out danger
I'd hammer out a warning
I'd hammer out love between my
    brothers and my sisters
All, all over this land.

If I had a bell I'd ring it in the morning,
I'd ring it in the evening all over this land
I'd ring out danger
I'd ring out a warning
I'd ring out love between my
    brothers and my sisters
All, all over this land.

If I had a song I'd sing it in the morning,
I'd sing it in the evening all over this land
I'd sing out danger
I'd sing out a warning
I'd sing out love between my
        brothers and my sisters
All, all over this land.

Well I got a hammer and I got a bell
And I got a song to sing all over this land
It's the hammer of justice
It's the bell of freedom
It's the song about love between my
        brothers and my sisters
All, all over this land.

It's the hammer of justice
It's the bell of freedom
It's the song about love between my
        brothers and my sisters
All, all over this land.

Superheroes!

We love superheroes! They capture our hearts and imagination with their daring, amazing, and heroic deeds. They fly, stretch, and swing through the air to save the world from destruction practically every day. Their superpowers amaze and delight us. Which one is your favorite?

Batman & Robin

Batman has no special powers, just a big brain, an undying hatred of criminals, and lots of cool toys. Rich playboy Bruce Wayne sees his parents get murdered when he is just a boy, and ever since then devotes his life to battling the criminal element in Gotham City. Aided by his sidekick, Robin, and their faithful butler, Alfred, as well as his gadgets—most famous, the Batmobile—Batman takes on his nemeses, including the Joker, Two-Face, the Penguin, and Catwoman.

Captain Marvel

Captain Marvel's origins are as a humanoid alien named Mar-Vell from a race called the Kree. With his powerful golden Nega-Bands (worn on the wrists), he is able to exchange atoms with teenager Rick Jones and take on human form. His powers, thanks to the extraordinary Nega-Bands, include superhuman strength, supersonic speed, and incredible stamina. On top of all that, he has a Cosmic Awareness that allows him to detect invisible beings, objects, and threats anywhere in the universe.

The Fantastic Four

The Fantastic Four are a band of friends who go out into space and come back with superpowers. Reed Richards is the scientist who builds the ship for their expedition; Sue Storm is his fiancée; Johnny Storm is her brother; and Ben Grimm is Reed's old friend.

In space, the four of them encounter a band of poisonous radiation, and when they crash back to earth, they find they have all been transformed. Reed, the leader of the team, becomes Mr. Fantastic. He can expand and stretch his body as if it were made of some kind of gum. Sue becomes the Invisible Girl, and can make herself and any objects she touches invisible. She also is capable of creating a form of mental shield, and has an endless supply of energy. Johnny Storm becomes the Human Torch, able to control fire, shoot it from his fingertips, and even fly through the air in a ball of flame. Ben becomes The Thing, a lumpy, rocky creature with a bad temper. His powers include the ability to withstand extreme heat and cold. Together they form the Fantastic Four.

Flash Gordon

Flash Gordon, an all-American athlete, is kidnapped from Earth and thrust into the middle of a raging war on the distant planet Mongo. Caught between the forces of Prince Barin, the rightful ruler of Mongo, and Ming the Merciless, self-proclaimed emperor of the universe, this ordinary man becomes a hero by displaying extraordinary courage. It is Dr. Hans Zarkov, one of the most brilliant scientists in the world, who forces Flash along with Dale Arden to accompany him on his spaceship to change the course of the approaching Mongo. Dr. Zarkov's scientific prowess has made him an invaluable ally in the fight against Ming. Under Flash's leadership, the oppressed people of Mongo are finally able to rise up and escape Ming's long reign of terror—a deed that Ming has sworn to avenge.

The Hulk

While supervising the trial for an experimental gamma bomb, Dr. Robert Bruce Banner, nuclear physicist, selflessly rushes to the rescue of a teenager who has wandered onto a testing field as the countdown nears zero. He pushes the teenager to safety but is caught in the gamma rays of the blast, and is permanently transformed. At first, Banner changes into a beastly Hulk at sunset and reverts to human form at dawn. After a while, his transformation into the childlike, green Hulk comes to be activated by the release of adrenaline whenever he is intensely excited, no matter what time of day. This 7-foot-tall, thousand-pound, green mass of fury possesses little of Banner's intelligence or memory, and is so easily enraged that he is a menace to society. You don't want to see him get angry!

Spiderman

Peter Parker, a.k.a. Spiderman, grows up in the house of his uncle Ben and aunt May. An ordinary teenager and a top student at school, Peter Parker gets saddled with superpowers when a radioactive spider bites him. From then on, Peter can climb the sides of buildings and swing through the city on long ropes of web that he shoots from his wrists. Perhaps his most important crime-fighting power is his "spider sense"—the ability to sense and anticipate danger. When a thief murders his uncle Ben during a crime that Spiderman could have prevented, he is racked with guilt. Remembering what his uncle Ben had told him—that with great power comes great responsibility—Spiderman vows to fight all evil until the end of his days. Among his many nemeses are Venom, Carnage, Kraven, and Green Goblin.

Superman

Sent to Earth from his collapsing home planet Krypton by his father, Superman is found and raised by the farmers Jonathan and Martha Kent—who name their new son Clark. Thanks to the Earth's sun, Clark has unbelievable powers. After realizing as a teenager that he is the strongest man on Earth, he uses his powers for good, and to help and protect innocent people!

As a young man, Clark moves to Metropolis, keeping his powers secret from every-body and leading a double life. As Clark Kent, he works for the Daily Planet, the biggest newspa-per. When he's not reporting on crime in the city of Metropolis, Kent/Superman is busy fighting it. Very little can stop the Man of Steel—except maybe Kryptonite.

Wonder Woman

Wonder woman is the daughter of Hippolyte, immortal Queen of the Amazons of Paradise Island. Hippolyte molds her daughter out of the clay of Paradise Island and names her Diana, after the Roman name for Artemis, goddess of the hunt. Diana is an exceptional child, displaying incredible strength and agility. She trains in a variety of skills including horsemanship, nursing, and "bullets and bracelets," an Amazon game where the player deflects projectiles with special bracelets.

When Hippolyte holds a contest to select an Amazon to travel to America as a champion of peace, Diana enters and defeats all the other contestants. Hippolyte endows her daughter with a costume and magical implements to represent her people in America. Her tools include her bracelets of submission, a lariat that forces complete honesty and obedience in anyone ensnared, and a jet that is visible only to the eyes of Amazons. With super strength, super speed, and Amazonian skills, Wonder woman is hugely successful in her mission from Amazon, routinely encountering and defeating agents of evil.

START A COLLECTION!

Starting a collection takes only a thirst for hunting down items and a passion for your hobby. Sometimes it doesn't even have to cost you a penny. You can collect just about anything—from action figures, autographs, and bottle caps, to marionettes, model trains, pez dispensers, and postcards.

COINS

Numismatics, or coin collecting, is a fascinating and fun hobby. Chances are you already have at least one or more "good luck coins"—some left-over foreign currency from a family vacation, a large penny, and maybe an old silver dollar—and therein the beginnings of a collection. Every coin tells a story, some of great leaders, history, royalty, power, and patriotism relating to their respective countries of origin. Famous figures come to life when depicted on an old coin. For example, Julius Caesar, Henry VIII, Napoleon, George Washington, Susan B. Anthony, and Abraham Lincoln are all portrayed on coins just as they appeared at the time.

It takes time, effort, and study to build a good collection. First decide what you want to collect—you can specialize in odd coins or unusual forms of money, or just focus on one coin type, like pennies, or the more rare two-cent pieces, three-cent pieces and twenty-cent pieces. It's up to you! You can even simply collect coins that catch your eye. Before spending money on your coin collection, read up on the subject, subscribe to a coin collecting magazine, and then attend a coin show.

BASEBALL CARDS

Professional baseball began in America in 1869, and by 1887 the first sets of baseball cards were available to baseball fans. For decades, baseball cards contained not just photos of the ballplayers, but illustrations as well. Most sports cards were originally items given out by tobacco companies to promote their products. In the 1930s, the tobacco was replaced by gum and the cards became more of the focus, as companies such as Goudey and Play Ball produced cards. It wasn't until after the Second World War that cards began to be produced by companies on a regular basis.

Collecting sports cards is a hobby that attracts collectors of all ages and incomes. You can start and build a collection for relatively little money, and when you are old and rich you can spend millions contributing to your collection!

Card prices vary: It is usually the desirability and statistics of the player that determines the value of the card. The rookie card, or first card of a particular player, is usually the most valuable card of that player. Hall of Fame players and record-breaking players will usually be harder and more expensive to attain.

COMIC BOOKS

When comic books first appeared in America, at the end of the 1800s, their purpose was mostly to amuse— that's why they're still called "comic," even though now you can find almost any type of story or art you could want.

By the 1930s, comic books got serious—and seriously fun! There were science-fiction stories, like *Flash Gordon*; detective stories, like *Dick Tracy*; and jungle adventures, like *Tarzan*. To build a comic book collection, there are a few things you should keep in mind. Your comic books will hold up best over time if you store them standing up (not stacked!) in their own plastic sleeves and cardboard backings, or in acid-free boxes. Also, early issues of almost any series are going to be the most valuable, so start soon! Last, get hold of a pricing guide. You'll want to know if that box your uncle gave you contains anything valuable—the most valuable comic, Action Comics #1, is worth $350,000!

GEORGE WASHINGTON (1732–99), known as the "Father of His Country," was born in Virginia, and later became the commander in chief of the Continental Army. After successfully leading his men to victory against the British in the Revolutionary War, he was unanimously elected the first president of the United States. His courage and noble judgment are embodied in a legend from his boyhood. The story goes that young George chopped down his father's prized cherry tree, and even though he faced being punished, he told the truth.

THOMAS JEFFERSON (1743–1826) was the third president of the U.S., but he is also remembered for being an imaginative inventor and architect. Before becoming president, though, he was the main author of the Declaration of Independence, which stated, "all men are created equal" with rights to "life, liberty, and the pursuit of happiness." Jefferson also was largely responsible for making sure that people would always be guaranteed freedom of speech, press, and religion in the Constitution.

ABRAHAM LINCOLN (1809–65) was born in a log cabin, but overcame his humble beginnings by studying and working hard to eventually become the sixteenth president. Shortly after he was elected, the Confederate Southern States left the Union, and the Civil War broke out. Under Lincoln's brave leadership, the country became whole again. He later signed the Emancipation Proclamation, which signaled the beginning of freedom for slaves. His most famous speech was the Gettysburg Address, which beautifully described his hopes for the rebirth of the nation.

FRANKLIN DELANO ROOSEVELT (1882–1945) became the thirty-second president, in 1933, when the United States was suffering through the Great Depression. Roosevelt had a radio show that he often used to calm people down, telling them, "The only thing

PRESIDENTIAL HEROES

we have to fear is fear itself." The president came up with the New Deal, a series of programs and agencies that helped the country get back on its feet again.

JOHN F. KENNEDY (1917–63) became the youngest president, at age 43, in 1961, but not before becoming a World War II hero and winning a Pulitzer Prize for his book *Profiles in Courage*. While in office, he fought for equal rights for African Americans and helped get the space program started. He led the way through some tense times with the Soviet Union and signed a treaty that helped limit the use of missiles and other weapons. Kennedy also was responsible for the Peace Corps, a popular volunteer organization that still brings education and skills to developing countries. His most famous quote is probably, "Ask not what your country can do for you; ask what you can do for your country."

George Washington's Tips on Manners

When George Washington was a teenager, in the early eighteenth century, he copied out 110 rules: "The Rules of Civility & Decent Behavior in Company and Conversation." They were a guide that would serve him well in his career as a diplomat and a leader—he was known for his impeccable manners. Some of the rules seem ridiculous now, but here are a few that, if followed today, would make for a much more considerate and pleasant society.

When in company, put not your hands to any part of the body not usually discovered.

 In the presence of others, sing not you yourself with a humming noise or drum with your fingers or feet.

 If you cough, sneeze, sigh, or yawn, do it not loud but privately; and speak not in your yawning, but put your handkerchief or hand before your face and turn aside.

 Shift not yourself in sight of others nor gnaw your nails.

 Keep your nails clean and short, also your hands and teeth clean, yet without showing any great concern for them.

Wear not your clothes foul, ript, or dusty, but see they be brush'd once every day at least and take heed that you approach not to any uncleanness.

 Think before you speak, pronounce not imperfectly, nor bring out your words too hastily, but distinctly.

 It's unbecoming to stoop much to one's meat. Keep your fingers clean & when foul wipe them on a corner of your table napkin.

 Put not another bit into your mouth till the former be swallowed. Let not your morsels be too big for the jowls.

 Drink not nor talk with your mouth full, neither gaze about you while you are drinking.

 Shake not your head, feet, or legs, roll not the eyes, lift not one eyebrow higher than the other, wry not the mouth, and bedew no man's face with your spittle by approaching too near him when you speak.

 Labour to keep alive in your breast that little spark of celestial fire called conscience.

A Bag
of Tools

by R. L. Sharpe

Isn't it strange
That princes and kings,
And clowns that caper
In sawdust rings,
And common people
Like you and me
Are builders for eternity?

Each is given a bag of tools,
A shapeless mass,
A book of rules;
And each must make—
Ere life is flown—
A stumbling block
Or a steppingstone.

Radio

You're probably aware by now that when you turn on the car radio, your favorite band isn't hidden in the glove compartment giving you a private concert. But have you ever wondered how your radio in fact works?

Radio waves are actually made of invisible light. The longest waves in the electromagnetic spectrum, they contain low-energy light (ultraviolet rays from the sun are an example of high-energy light). These invisible waves are all around you on a constant basis. They are used to carry signals for all sorts of things you use every day: radios, televisions, cordless and cellular phones, garage door openers, baby monitors, and even your favorite remote-control car.

In the case of radios, the program you listen to, whether it is music or talk, originates in a sound booth. The disc jockey speaks into his microphone, which converts the sound waves into an electrical signal. This signal is again converted, this time to an audio wave plus a carrier wave. It is amplified and sent to the station's antenna. The converted signal stimulates the atoms in the antenna, and their electrons begin to give off invisible light that spreads into the sky.

Your radio has an antenna of its own that catches these waves because you are "tuned in" to the station. (Note: A tuner enables your radio to separate out and select the correct waves of your station from the thousands your antenna is receiving at any given moment.)

The signal that was converted at the station so it could travel to your radio is now converted back. Your speakers act as a reverse microphone, turning the electrical audio signal back into sound waves so you can hear your program loud and clear!

Light Bulbs

Light bulbs—we use them every day to see the world around us. But how do they work? Well, an incandescent light bulb is composed of a glass bulb filled with inert gas (usually argon), a coiled wire filament, and electrical contact wires. The filament wire is made out of tungsten. It has an extremely high melting point. When an electrical current is delivered to the filament via the electrical contact wires, the filament heats up so much that it glows. This is what we see as light.

The reduced-pressure inert gas is there to keep the metal from mixing with oxygen in the air, which would cause the tungsten wire to burn out. When a filament does burn out, it is because over time the tungsten wire vaporizes. The black dust that settles on the inside of the glass is the resolidified tungsten metal.

The problem with incandescent light bulbs is that the heat wastes a lot of electricity. Heat is not light, and energy spent creating heat in order to create light is a waste.

A florescent bulb uses a different method to produce light. An electric current is passed through mercury vapor in the florescent tube. The vapor emits ultraviolet rays that hit the phosphor coating on the inside of the tube. The phosphor emits white light. A fluorescent bulb produces less heat, so it is much more efficient. A 15-watt fluorescent bulb will produce the same amount of light as a 60-watt incandescent bulb.

HOMONYMS

Are you a jokester? Do you love puns—that is, plays on words with the same or similar sounds? Then you are probably already a fan of the homonym, a word that has multiple meanings. Here is a joke that makes use of homonyms: What do you get when you feed a cat a lemon? A sour puss. The punch line contains two homonyms. "Sour," which can mean "tart" or "bad-tempered," and "puss," which can mean "cat" or "face." See if you can discover the double meanings of the homonyms (in bold) in the following jokes:

Why did Ethan throw the butter up in the air?

He wanted to see **butter fly** *(butterfly).*

What do you call a zipper on an orange?

A fruit **fly**.

What did the big flower say to the little flower?

"Hey, **bud**.*"*

What part of the gym is never the same?

The **changing** *rooms.*

HOMOPHONES

As anyone trying to master English as a second language can tell you, homophones—words that sound alike but have different meanings—are slippery business. In fact, they can be difficult even for native speakers. Here are a few common examples: brake and break; hoarse and horse; knight and night; moose and mousse; plain and plane; sea and see. See if you can fill in the blanks of these sentences that use homophones:

After the rain stopped, a multicolored _____ of light filled the sky over Noah's _____ .

The show horse had been trotting but changed its _____ just before jumping over the _____ .

The distinguished army _____ laughed when his niece told him he had a corn _____ stuck between his teeth.

"How could it _____?" asked Billy. "Gretchen is such a poor speller, yet she won the spelling _____?"

(Answers: arc, ark; gait, gate; colonel, kernel; be, bee)

Word Fun!

MY SHIP SAILS

Ahoy!

Number of players: four to seven

Setup: The oldest player is the dealer. He deals out seven cards to each player (the extra cards aren't used). Players then arrange their cards by suit (for example, all spades together) and decide which suit they're going to try and collect (they can change their minds as many times as they want, though).

Goal: To be the first to collect seven cards of the same suit

How to play: Each player takes a card he doesn't want and passes it to the right. Cards keep getting passed until someone collects seven cards of the same suit, and yells out, "My ship sails!"

CRAZY EIGHTS

The original "Uno"

Number of players: two to five

Setup: Deal out seven cards to each player and leave the rest facedown in a stack. Take one card from the top of the stack and place it faceup on the table. This will be the discard pile.

Goal: To be the first to get rid of all your cards

How to play: The player to the dealer's left goes first. He looks through his hand for a card that matches the one on the discard pile, either in value (for example, both are Jacks) or suit (both are spades). If he finds one, he places it on top of the discard pile. If the player doesn't have a card that matches, he draws from the deck until he gets one that does match. The exception: Eights are "wild cards"-meaning that you may play them on any card. Whoever plays an 8 of any suit gets to choose the next suit to be played. The winner is the player who gets rid of all his cards first, but the game may continue until there's only one player left standing.

ery finished it begins a new suit. The first player to run out of cards collects all the jellybeans in the pot. Play as many "rounds" as you like, and the winner is the one with the most jellybeans at the end.

CARD GAMES

PLAY OR PAY

Who'll get the pot?

Number of players: three to five

Supplies: twenty jellybeans (or toothpicks, buttons, beads, etc.) per player

Setup: The dealer hands out twenty jellybeans to each player, and then deals out the entire deck of cards (it doesn't matter if some players have more cards than others).

Goal: To collect the most jellybeans

How to play: The player to the dealer's left picks a card from his hand and puts it faceup on the table. The player to his left then has to play the next card in the sequence. For example, if the first player played a 3 of spades, the next player has to play the 4 of spades. If a player doesn't have the next card in the sequence, he puts a jellybean into the pot, and it becomes the next player's turn. When the entire suit is played (the card following a King is the Ace of the same suit), the player who finished it begins a new suit. The first player to run out of cards collects all the jellybeans in the pot. Play as many "rounds" as you like, and the winner is the one with the most jellybeans at the end.

OLD MAID

Don't get stuck with the old fuddy-duddy.

Number of players: three to five

Setup: Remove the Queen of clubs, the Queen of diamonds, and the Queen of spades. Deal out all the cards to the players (it doesn't matter if some players have more than others).

Goal: To avoid becoming the "Old Maid"

How to play: If any player has a pair of matching cards (such as two 7s or two Kings), he discards them on the table. The player to the dealer's left fans out his cards so nobody can see them. He offers them to the player on his left, who pulls one out of the fan without seeing what it is and adds it to his hand. If it makes a pair with anything he has, he discards the pair. That player then lets the next player pick a card from his

174

hand in the same way. The game continues until the only card left is the Queen of hearts, the Old Maid. The player left holding the Old Maid is the loser!

SPIT

A game of speed.

Number of players: two

Setup: Deal out all the cards to both players. Players arrange their cards into five stacks, facedown and solitaire-style (from right to left, the first pile has one card, the second has two, the third has three, and so forth). Turn the top card of each stack faceup. If any top cards match (say two Jacks or three 4s), the player can put them together in a separate stack and turn the next cards up. Each

player places his leftover cards in a pile in the middle.

Goal: To be the first to get rid of all your cards

How to play: Players flip over the top cards from their leftover piles into the middle space between them. These are the

"spit" piles. The players then try to get rid of all of their cards from their five stacks into these spit piles as fast as they can, in sequence. Numbers can go up or down (2-3-2-A-K). As each player places faceup cards onto the center piles, the next facedown cards on their stacks are turned faceup. Matching cards can be placed together, and if any stack is finished, a faceup card from another stack can be moved into the empty space, and the card beneath it turned up. (Players are allowed five cards facing up.) If at any time neither player can put any more cards onto the spit piles, both players take the next cards from their leftover piles and place them on their spit piles. When one player has finished all of his stacks, he quickly slaps the spit pile he thinks has fewer cards and takes possession of it-if the other player notices, he can try to slap it first. The players then set up all of their cards again in solitaire-style stacks, and the next round begins. The game ends when one player has discarded all his cards.

Virtual Vesuvius

There are 139 active volcanoes in North and Central America—that's more than anywhere else in the world. Some, like Mount St. Helens in Washington State, erupt once every few hundred years, covering hundreds of miles in volcanic ash. Others, like Kilauea in Hawaii have continuous non-explosive eruptions. The lava bubbles, coughs, and hisses every day. Even if you don't live near an active volcano, you can build one in your backyard with common household ingredients. How often it blows its top will be up to you.

This can be a very messy project, so ask an adult for permission before you get started. Then gather some friends and do this one outdoors for best results.

Large narrow-neck bottle, large aluminum baking tray, bubble-wrap, tape, self-drying clay, pebbles, twigs, tempera paints, paintbrushes, dried moss or lichen, glue, baking soda, paper cup, liquid dish soap, distilled vinegar, red food coloring

1. Stand the bottle in the middle of the tray. To begin building your volcano shape, form a cone by taping bubble wrap around the bottle. Do not cover the opening of the bottle. Make sure the smooth side of the bubble wrap faces out.
2. Cover the cone with clay all the way to the lip of the bottle. Mold the clay around the bottle opening to resemble a volcanic crater.

3. Press twigs and pebbles into the clay to represent trees and lava rocks. When the clay has dried, paint the surface with tempera. Then, once the paint is dry, attach moss and lichen to the surface with glue.
4. When you are ready for your volcano to erupt, pour two tablespoons of baking soda into the mouth of the bottle.
5. In a paper cup, mix about a tablespoon of liquid dish soap and about 4 ounces of vinegar. Add a few drops of red food coloring.
6. Pour the liquid mixture into the mouth of the bottle. Then stand back and watch your molten lava spew!

Note: Once the baking soda has dried completely, you can add more vinegar solution to make the volcano erupt again.

In the town where I was born
Lived a man who sailed to sea.
And he told us of his life
In the land of submarines.

So we sailed up to the sun
Till we found the sea of green.
And we lived beneath the waves
In our yellow submarine.

(Chorus)

And our friends are all on board,
Many more of them live next door.
And the band begins to play.

(Chorus)

As we live a life of ease
Every one of us has all we need.
Sky of blue and sea of
Green in our yellow submarine.

We all live in a yellow submarine,
Yellow submarine, yellow submarine.
We all live in a yellow submarine,
Yellow submarine, yellow submarine.

Nine-year-old Peter Hatcher's little brother Fudge makes Peter's life miserable. He causes trouble and embarrassment wherever he goes. Fudge makes Peter feel like a "Fourth Grade Nothing." What is worse, Peter's parents think Fudge's antics are adorable. They are always fussing over him and giving him more attention than they give poor Peter. So when Fudge messes with Peter's pet turtle, Dribble, it's the last straw! Judy Blume is the author of more than two dozen books, including three follow-up books to *Tales of a Fourth Grade Nothing* (1972): *Superfudge* (1980), *Fudge-a-Mania* (1990), and *Double Fudge* (2002). Her books have sold more than 75 million copies, and have been translated into dozens of languages. In 1996, Blume received the American Library Association's prestigious Margaret A. Edwards Award for Lifetime Achievement.

I will never forget Friday, May tenth. It's the most important day of my life. It didn't start out that way. It started out ordinary. I went to school. I ate my lunch. I had gym. And then I walked home from school with Jimmy Fargo. We planned to meet at our special rock in the park as soon as we changed our clothes.

In the elevator I told Henry I was glad summer was coming. Henry said he was too. When I got out at my floor I walked down the hall and opened the door to my apartment. I took off my jacket and hung it in the closet. I put my books on the hall table next to my mother's purse. I went straight to my room to change my clothes and check Dribble.

The first thing I noticed was my chain latch. It was unhooked. My bedroom door was open. And there was a chair smack in the middle of my doorway. I nearly tumbled over it. I ran to my dresser to check Dribble. He wasn't there! His bowl with the rocks and water was there—but Dribble was gone.

Tales of a Fourth Grade Nothing

by
Judy Blume

I got really scared. I thought, *Maybe he died while I was at school and I didn't know about it.* So I rushed into the kitchen and hollered, "Mom . . . where's

Dribble?" My mother was baking something. My brother sat on the kitchen floor, banging pots and pans together. "Be quiet!" I yelled at Fudge. "I can't hear anything with all that noise."

"What did you say, Peter?" my mother asked me.

"I said I can't find Dribble. Where is he?"

"You mean he's not in his bowl?" my mother asked.

I shook my head.

"Oh dear!" my mother said. "I hope he's not crawling around somewhere. You know I don't like the way he smells. I'm going to have a look in the bedrooms. You check in here, Peter."

My mother hurried off. I looked at my brother. He was smiling. "Fudge, do you know where Dribble is?" I asked calmly.

Fudge kept smiling.

"Did you take him? Did you, Fudge?" I asked not so calmly.

Fudge giggled and covered his mouth with his hands.

I yelled. "Where is he? What did you do with my turtle?"

No answer from Fudge. He banged his pots and pans together again. I yanked the pots out of his hand. I tried to speak softly. "Now tell me where Dribble is. Just tell me where my turtle is. I won't be mad if you tell me. Come on, Fudge . . . please."

Fudge looked up at me. "In tummy," he said.

"What do you mean, in tummy?" I asked, narrowing my eyes.

> "Where is he? What did you do with my turtle?"

"Dribble in tummy!" He repeated.

"What tummy?" I shouted at my brother.

"This one," Fudge said, rubbing his stomach. "Dribble in this tummy! Right here!"

I decided to go along with his game. "Okay. How did he get in there, Fudge?" I asked.

Fudge stood up. He jumped up and down and sang out, "I ATE HIM . . . ATE HIM . . . ATE HIM!" Then he ran out of the room.

My mother came back into the kitchen. "Well, I just can't find him anywhere," she said. "I looked in all the dresser drawers and the bathroom cabinets and the shower and the tub and. . . ."

"Mom," I said, shaking my head. "How could you?"

"How could I what, Peter?" Mom asked.

"How could you let him do it?"

"Let who do what, Peter?" Mom asked.

"LET FUDGE EAT DRIBBLE!" I screamed.

My mother started to mix whatever she was baking. "Don't be silly, Peter," she said. "Dribble is a turtle."

"HE ATE DRIBBLE!" I insisted.

"Peter Warren Hatcher! STOP SAYING THAT!" Mom hollered.

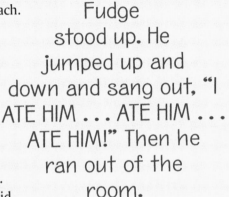

Fudge stood up. He jumped up and down and sang out, "I ATE HIM . . . ATE HIM . . . ATE HIM!" Then he ran out of the room.

"Well, ask him. Go ahead and ask him," I told her.

Fudge was standing in the kitchen doorway with a big grin on his face. My mother picked him up and patted his head. "Fudgie," she said to him, "tell Mommy where brother's turtle is."

"In tummy," Fudge said.

"What tummy?" Mom asked.

"MINE!" Fudge laughed.

My mother put Fudge down on the kitchen counter where he couldn't get away from her. "Oh, you're fooling Mommy . . . right?"

"No fool!" Fudge said.

My mother turned very pale. "You really ate your brother's turtle?"

Big smile from Fudge.

"YOU MEAN THAT YOU PUT HIM IN YOUR MOUTH AND CHEWED HIM UP . . . LIKE THIS?" Mom made believe she was chewing.

"No," Fudge said.

A smile of relief crossed my mother's face. "Of course you didn't. It's just a joke." She put Fudge down on the floor and gave me a look.

Fudge babbled. "No chew. No chew. Gulp . . . gulp . . . all gone turtle. Down Fudge's tummy."

Me and my mother stared at Fudge.

"You didn't!" Mom said.

> "YOU MEAN THAT YOU PUT HIM IN YOUR MOUTH AND CHEWED HIM UP . . . LIKE THIS?" Mom made believe she was chewing.

"Did so!" Fudge said.

"No!" Mom shouted.

"Yes!" Fudge shouted back.

"Yes?" Mom asked weakly, holding onto a chair with both hands.

"Yes!" Fudge beamed.

My mother moaned and picked up my brother. "Oh no! My angel! My precious little baby! OH . . . NO. . . ."

My mother didn't stop to think about my turtle. She didn't even give Dribble a thought. She didn't even stop to wonder how my turtle liked being swallowed by my brother. She ran to the phone with Fudge tucked under one arm. I followed. Mom dialed the operator and cried, "Oh help! This is an emergency. My baby ate a turtle . . . STOP THAT LAUGHING," my mother told the operator. "Send an ambulance right away; 25 West 68th Street."

Mom hung up. She didn't look too well. Tears were running down her face. She put Fudge down on the floor. I couldn't understand why she was so upset. Fudge seemed just fine.

"Help me, Peter," Mom begged. "Get me blankets."

I ran into my brother's room. I grabbed two blankets from Fudge's bed. He was following me around with that silly grin on his face. I felt like giving him a pinch. How could he stand there looking so happy when he had my turtle inside him?

I delivered the blankets to my mother. She wrapped Fudge up in them and ran to the front door. I followed and grabbed her purse from the hall table. I figured she'd be glad I thought of that.

Out in the hall I pressed the elevator buzzer. We had to wait a few minutes. Mom paced up and down in front of the elevator. Fudge was cradled in her arms. He sucked his fingers and made that slurping noise I like. But all I could think of was Dribble.

Finally, the elevator got to our floor. There were three people in it besides Henry. "This is an emergency," Mom wailed. "The ambulance is waiting downstairs. Please hurry!"

"Yes, Mrs. Hatcher. Of course," Henry said. "I'll run her down just as fast as I can. No other stops."

Someone poked me in the back. I turned around. It was Mrs. Rudder. "What's the matter?" she whispered.

"It's my brother," I whispered back. "He ate my turtle."

> "What's the matter?" she whispered. "It's my brother," I whispered back. "He ate my turtle."

Mrs. Rudder whispered that to the man next to her and he whispered it to the lady next to him who whispered it to Henry. I faced front and pretended I didn't hear anything.

My mother turned around with Fudge in her arms and said, "That's not funny. Not funny at all!"

But Fudge said, "Funny, funny, funny Fudgie!"

Everybody laughed. Everybody except my mother.

The elevator door opened. Two men, dressed in white, were waiting with a stretcher. "This the baby?" one of them asked.

"Don't worry, lady. We'll be to the hospital in no time."

"Yes. Yes, it is," Mom sobbed.

"Don't worry, lady. We'll be to the hospital in no time."

"Come, Peter," my mother said, tugging at my sleeve. "We're going to ride in the ambulance with Fudge."

My mother and I climbed into the back of the blue ambulance. I was never in one before. It was neat. Fudge kneeled on a cot and peered out through the window. He waved at the crowd of people that had gathered on the sidewalk.

One of the attendants sat in back with us. The other one was driving. "What seems to be the trouble, lady?" the attendant asked. "This kid looks pretty healthy to me."

"He swallowed a turtle," my mother whispered.

"He did WHAT?" the attendant asked.

"Ate my turtle. That's what!" I told him.

My mother covered her face with her hanky and started to cry again.

"Hey, Joe!" the attendant called to the driver. "Make it snappy . . . *this* one swallowed a turtle!"

"That's not funny!" Mom insisted. I didn't think so either, considering it was my turtle!

We arrived at the back door of the hospital. Fudge was whisked away by two nurses. My mother ran after him. "You wait here, young man," another nurse called to me, pointing to a bench.

I sat down on the hard, wooden bench. I didn't have anything to do. There weren't any books or magazines spread out, like when I go to Dr. Cone's office. So I watched the clock and read all the signs on the walls. I found out I was in the emergency section of the hospital.

After a while the nurse came back. She gave me some paper and crayons. "Here you are. Be a good boy and draw some pictures. Your mother will be out soon."

I wondered if she knew about Dribble and that's why she was trying to be nice to me. I didn't feel like drawing any pictures. I wondered what they were doing to Fudge in there. Maybe he wasn't such a bad little guy after all. I remembered that Jimmy Fargo's little cousin once swallowed the most valuable rock from Jimmy's collection. And my mother told me that when I was a little kid I swallowed a quarter. Still . . . a quarter's not like a turtle!

I watched the clock on the wall for an hour and ten minutes. Then a door opened and my mother stepped out with Dr. Cone. I was surprised to see him. I didn't know he worked in the hospital.

"Hello, Peter," he said.

"Hello, Dr. Cone. Did you get my turtle?"

"Not yet, Peter," he said. "But I do have something to show you. Here are some X-rays of your brother." I studied the X-rays as Dr. Cone pointed things out to me.

"You see," he said. "There's your turtle . . . right there."

I looked hard. "Will Dribble be in there forever?" I asked.

"No. Definitely not! We'll get him out. We gave Fudge some medicine already. That should do the trick nicely."

"What kind of medicine?" I asked. "What trick?"

"Castor oil, Peter," my mother said. "Fudge took castor oil. And milk of magnesia. And prune juice too. Lots of that. All those things will help to get Dribble out of Fudge's tummy."

"We just have to wait," Dr. Cone said. "Probably until tomorrow or the day after. Fudge will have to spend the night here. But I don't think he's going to be swallowing anything that he isn't supposed to be swallowing from now on."

"How about Dribble?" I asked. "Will Dribble be all right?" My mother and Dr. Cone looked at each other. I knew the answer before he shook his head and said, "I think you may have to get a new turtle, Peter."

"I don't want a new turtle!" I said. Tears came to my eyes. I was embarrassed and wiped them away with the back of my hand. Then my nose started to run and I had to sniffle. "I want Dribble," I said. "That's the only turtle I want."

"You see," he said. "There's your turtle . . . right there." I looked hard. "Will Dribble be in there forever?" I asked.

If you are on the Gloomy Line,
    Get a transfer.
If you're inclined to fret and pine,
    Get a transfer.
Get off the track of doubt and gloom,
Get on the Sunshine Track—there's room—
    Get a transfer.

If you're on the Worry Train,
    Get a transfer.
You must not stay there and complain,
    Get a transfer.
The Cheerful Cars are passing through,
And there's lots of room for you—
    Get a transfer.

If you're on the Grouchy Track,
    Get a transfer.
Just take a Happy Special back,
    Get a transfer.
Jump on the train and pull the rope,
That lands you at the station Hope—
    Get a transfer.

Get A Transfer

Anonymous

DOCTOR, DOCTOR

A man walks into a doctor's office and says, "Doctor, Doctor, I think I need glasses." "You certainly do," replies the doctor. "This is a hamburger stand!"

A man walks into a psychiatrist's office and says, "Doctor, you've got to help me. I think I'm a dog!" The psychiatrist replies, "Just lie down here on the couch and tell me all about it." "I can't. I'm not allowed on the furniture!"

"Doctor, Doctor, I have cucumbers growing out of my ears!" "How did this happen?" "Beats me— I planted carrots."

Whad'ya call a boy people walk all over?

Matt.

Whad'ya call a boy who's always asking you for money?

Bill.

Whad'ya call a boy who floats on water?

Bob.

Whad'ya call a boy with a shovel?

Doug.

Whad'ya call a boy without a shovel?

Douglas.

WHAD'YA CALL?

Waiter, what's this fly
doing in my soup?
            "Hmm, looks like
        the backstroke to me."

Waiter, what's this fly
doing in my soup?
        "I think it's drowning, sir."

Waiter, there's a fly
in my soup!
        Okay, I'll bring you a fork.

"Waiter, there's a fly
in my soup!
        That's funny. There were
    two when I left the kitchen.

Waiter, there's a fly
in my soup!
            Yes sir, we ran
            out of spiders.

Waiter, there's a *dead* fly
in my soup!
            "Yes sir, it's the hot
        water that kills them."

Waiter, there's a fly
in my soup!
            "That's *not* a fly sir,
            that's just dirt in
            the shape of a fly."

WAITER, THERE'S A FLY IN MY SOUP

A Boy's Best Friend

Pet Trivia

IGUANAS have a dozen or so large pores on the undersides of their thighs. These pores secrete a waxy substance that they use to mark their territory and identify one another.

HAMSTERS get their name from the German word *hamstern*, which means "to hoard" or "to forage," because they store food in their cheeks, which puff out enormously!

Though you could probably tell by looking at it, the GUINEA PIG is not a pig. It doesn't come from New Guinea, either! They were probably called "pigs" for their grunts and squeals, and they may have been sold by British sailors, who brought them back from South America in the 1600s, for a guinea (a form of English currency).

A DOG wags its tail as a way of talking and telling you he is feeling happy. A dog may also wag its tail as a way of communicating with other dogs— one wag might indicate "Hello, how are you?" while another wag might say "I'm the boss around here."

Have you ever heard of a DEGU? Degus are rodents from Chile that, like some lizards, have the ability to shed their tails if they're caught. Degus, however, will never grow a new one, and their ability to balance will never be the same.

Earth's first space traveler was a DOG!

Did you know that ferrets are as smart as dogs?

In the wild, IGUANAS like to hang out on tree branches over ponds and streams. This way, if they feel threatened, they simply drop into the water and swim to safety.

You can tell the age of a young TURTLE by looking at its shell, but not an old turtle. The top of a turtle's shell is divided into sections called shields. On each shield are little circles. In a young turtle, each circle stands for a year's growth—e.g., a two-year-old turtle has two circles

The oldest goldfish on record died at the ripe old age of forty-one.

Exotic Pets

BIG CATS: While some people are daring enough to keep tigers, lions, or other huge cats around, those animals need more raw meat than your grocery store can probably handle, and even when they're playing, their size alone makes them quite dangerous. However, some wildcats can be tamed, if you have the money, the space, and the patience! Cats like caracals, servals, bobcats, and lynxes can be trained to use the litter box and get along with other pets just fine.

FERRETS: If a ferret isn't a weasel, and it isn't a rodent, then what is it? Ferrets are totally domesticated animals that are related to (and act a lot like) weasels, which live in the wild. They are as intelligent as dogs and make lively, playful, frisky little friends, but have mischievous, weasely habits—they love to steal things.

POTBELLIED PIGS: Believe it or not, pigs are very clean animals. They get overheated easily, which is why they're fond of rolling around in the mud. As pets, pigs are smart, can be trained, and can go anywhere with you, just like a dog. However, potbellied pigs grow to be 150 pounds and will knock over anything that isn't nailed down!

IGUANAS: Iguanas may be beautiful, but they sure aren't cuddly. These spiky green reptiles will hang out with the family like the average cat, but need lots more care. For one thing, they are used to hot jungle climates with plenty of places to go swimming. Iguana owners have to provide special lights to keep their pets warm. For another thing, they grow to be about six feet long from end to end, and need lots of space. Many iguana owners devote a whole room to their reptile!

Rabbits should never be picked up by their ears. Ow!

on each shield. After five or ten years, however, you can no longer determine a turtle's age by the circles as they have either become too crowded or have begun to wear off.

Just like cats, RABBITS can get hairballs from grooming themselves—but unlike cats, they can't get rid of them. Feeding your rabbit fresh pineapple juice or pineapple chunks can help prevent hairballs: Pineapple contains an enzyme that helps rabbits digest the hair.

SNAKES can't really be charmed. In India, men called snake charmers play music for cobra snakes, and the cobras seem to dance to it. But in fact snakes are actually deaf. Snake charmers sway and tap on the ground as they play music and the snake feels the vibrations and gets excited, rearing up to strike the charmer. When a cobra is ready to strike, it watches the victim carefully and follows the victim's movements—hence it appears to be swaying to the music.

Some pet rats can be taught to respond to their names.

Pet Posterity

TURTLES: The red-eared slider, which is the most common pet turtle, can live to be 40 years old!

DOGS: In general, the bigger the breed, the shorter its life span. The smallest dogs can live to be 18, and large dogs about 11 or 12.

CATS: The oldest cat on record was 36 when he died in 1936, but that's quite unusual. However, a healthy indoor cat can easily live to be 20.

RABBITS: Most rabbits kept in a safe and clean environment can live to be 10.

LIZARDS: Some lizards, like geckos, can live to be 20.

RODENTS: Gerbils and Syrian (golden) hamsters usually live 2–3 years. Mice live 1–3 years, rats can live 2–4 years, and guinea pigs live the longest— 5–7 years.

FISH: Goldfish can live to be 25, if well taken care of.

Questions

Why do bulls get angry at the color red?
Actually, they don't. Bulls are believed to be colorblind. What makes them angry in a bullfight is not the color red but the movement of the cape.

If chimpanzees are so similar to us, why can't they speak?
Chimpanzees are unable to talk the way we do because their vocal cords are located higher in their throats than human beings'. They also are unable to produce the range of different sounds required for human speech. However, chimps are highly intelligent animals (we share approximately 98 percent of the same genes with them), and we've helped them learn to communicate with us through sign language and other systems that use symbols.

Just how smart are parrots?
All parrots are extremely intelligent. The larger parrots (such as the African Grey) have an IQ approximately equal to a four- or five-year-old child and have the emotional development of a two-year-old.

These birds not only have learned to mimic human speech, but also can reproduce sounds. Certain parrots, such as the African Grey, can learn hundreds of words and have the ability to express themselves, creating different combinations of words.

Parrots are highly social, active, and sensitive animals that need a great deal of attention and care when they are kept as pets.

Are dogs colorblind?
Dogs can see colors, but to a very limited degree. They can tell the difference between yellow and blue but not red and green. A dog's vision is dichromatic, which means they can only distinguish between two colors: blue and yellow (or yellowish green).

Most people's vision is trichromatic, which means we can differentiate among red, blue, yellow, and yellowish green. Domesticated dogs and cats lost most of their color sight because they no longer have to hunt during the day. The big wildcats, for example, still have cones (color sight) because they must hunt in broad daylight in order to survive. Housecats (and dogs) see extremely well at night due to their ability to perceive the gray scale, and can catch little nocturnal varmints. Smaller dog breeds often were developed as ratters, and small, tame cats have been used on ships as mousers for hundreds of years.

How did the ladybug get its name?

It's said that during the Middle Ages, a group of farmers prayed to the Virgin Mary for help when swarms of aphids began destroying their crops. Since ladybugs love to feast on these little devils, Mary answered the farmer's prayers by sending them these brightly colored bugs, which gladly ate all the pests, saving the harvest! In honor of the Virgin, the farmers named the beetles "Beetles of Our Lady," hence the name "ladybugs."

How did the killer whale get its name?

Killer whales, or orcas, (Orcinus orca) are the major predators of the ocean. Their diet consists mainly of other marine life: from small fish to sharks to even other whales. They've even been known to

attack great whites. It is believed the name "killer whale" is a shortened version of "killer of whales," which originated with the fisherman who witnessed orcas feeding on other whales. Killer whales are technically not whales, but are in fact the largest member of the dolphin family.

Why does the chameleon change color?

Many animals, like the chameleon, are not equipped to fight their enemies, and therefore need to hide from them. The chameleon can change color amazingly fast. When on the ground its body is green with yellow spots and it has bright yellow legs. When it is in the trees it turns completely green to blend in with its surroundings.

Can fish survive out of water?

Most fish will die if removed from water; yet the lungfish of Africa, Australia, and South America often spends long periods out of water. Its body is adapted to breathe air, and during periods of drought the lungfish digs a hole in the mud. Slime from its body forms a protective cocoon until the water returns.

LEAP FROG

How high can you go?

Number of players: two or more

What you need: a large open area

Everybody stands in a straight line with at least two arms' lengths of space in between each person. Each player crouches in frog position by bending at the knees. Evenly distribute your weight between your hands and feet. Make sure you all have your heads down. Start with the "frog" at the end of the line. He places his hands on the back of the frog in front of him, and leaps over that person with his legs on either side of him. He continues down the line until he's jumped over everybody. Then the new last frog begins jumping, and so on.

Fun & Games

SARDINES

Hide-and-seek, but funnier!

Number of players: four or more

What you need: Inside or defined outside space with good hiding spots

Only one person hides. The other players count to a hundred and then search. The first person to find the hider squeezes into the same spot and keeps quiet. The second person to find the hider does the same and so on until only one player is left seeking. The trick is make yourself as skinny as possible and not laugh!

CAPTURE THE FLAG

Get the flag and go!

Number of players: six or more

What you need: 2 white flags, a large open area to run in (a soccer field is ideal), tape or chalk to mark boundaries

The object of the game is to capture the other team's flag. Mark the side and end lines of the field, a dividing line in the middle, two endzones, and a jail near each endzone. Place a flag in each endzone. Divide players into two teams. Each team occupies their half of the field. Players must run through the opposing team's territory, grab their flag, and get it back across the midline without being tagged. Tagged players must go to jail. Jailed players must stay in jail unless they are tagged by an untagged teammate and freed. Players are not allowed to hang out at their endzones guarding their flag. Game is over when a flag is captured or if all of a team's players are in jail.

Joy to the World

by Hoyt Axton

Jeremiah was a bullfrog,
Was a good friend of mine.
Never understood a single word he said,
But I helped him a-drinkin' his wine.
Yes, he always had some mighty fine wine.

(Chorus)

Singing joy to the world.

All the boys and girls now.

Joy to the fishes in the deep blue sea.

Joy to you and me.

If I were the king of the world,
Tell you what I'd do.
Throw away the cars and the bars
    and the wars,
And make sweet love to you.
Yes, I'd make sweet love to you.

(Chorus)

You know I love the ladies,
Love to have my fun.
I'm a high night flyer
    and a rainbow rider,
A straight shootin' son of a gun.
Yes, a straight shootin' son of a gun.

(Chorus)

205

Worm Farm

Imagine having five hearts, eating your weight in food every day, breathing through your skin, and spending most of your time digging around in dirt. That's what it's like to be a worm. These wriggly critters have the Midas touch with garbage. They can turn it into nitrogen-rich soil, which is worth its weight in gold to plants, gardeners, and farmers. You can turn your old apple peels and egg-shells into "pay dirt" with a little help from some night crawlers that you care for in a worm farm.

Lidded container (preferably plastic) about 18-inches wide x 12 inches long x 12 inches high, newspaper, bowl of water, soil, food scraps, large stirring stick, a dozen or more red worms (also called red wigglers or night crawlers) found outdoors among decomposing leaves or at a bait shop

1. Ask a parent to poke several small holes in the lid and sides of your container for air.
2. Rip several pages of newspaper into strips and soak in a bowl of water. Squeeze the excess water out of the paper and fill your bin about halfway.
3. Sprinkle a thin layer of soil on top of the damp newspaper.
4. Add small scraps of food to the bin and turn the mixture over a few times (do this every time you add food).
5. Add your worms. Keep your bin in a cool spot away from direct sunlight, like the basement or garage. Make sure the bedding stays moist but not soggy.
6. Watch the worms do their stuff. Feed them a little bit every day, or a few times

a week. Avoid overfeeding by checking to see that the worms have eaten food scraps before giving them more. You'll know you're not feeding them enough if they look pale and stringy.

Worm Juice

After a month or so, the worm bedding turns into humus, a natural fertilizer that comes from the worms' liquid and solid waste. You can harvest the humus by feeding the worms on one side of the bin for a while. They'll migrate to that side, and you can remove the humus using a big spoon or scoop. Repeat steps 2 and 3 to refill this side of your

bin. Start feeding on the "new" side again to entice your worms so you can harvest the other side also. Humus is rich stuff, so you don't need much to fertilize your soil.

Happy Meals

DO feed your worms coffee grounds and filters, tea bags, fruit and vegetable scraps, eggshells, cereal, bread

DON'T feed your worms onions, garlic, meat, fat, grease, dairy, or non-organic matter

Gone Fishin'

Worms reproduce every few weeks. So, before long, you'll have plenty of bait to go catch the big one.

ome of the best things in life come in bite sizes. This ultimate recipe for nachos ups the ante for plain old chips & dip. Served hot with beans and melted cheese, it's practically a meal unto itself. Potato skins are equally good, and you can spice them up with a dash of red pepper sauce or salsa. For larger snack appetites, sink your teeth into Cheesy Pizza Bread. And for a hot snack that you don't have to bake, try these flavored popcorn recipes. Just right for a night at home watching movies.

CHEESY POTATO SKINS

2 medium-size baking potatoes
2 tablespoons butter, softened
1 cup cheddar cheese, grated
4 slices bacon, cooked and crumbled
$1/4$ cup sour cream
2 tablespoons black olives, chopped
2 tablespoons chives, finely chopped (optional)

1. Preheat oven to 425°F.
2. Scrub potatoes well and pierce with a fork. Bake on bottom rack for 1 hour, or until tender when tested with fork. Let potatoes cool enough to handle.
3. Cut potatoes in half lengthwise. With large spoon, scoop out center of each potato, leaving a shell thickness of about $1/2$ inch. (store scooped-out potato in container for another use).
4. Quarter potato halves. Then cut quarters in half to create sixteen triangular wedges. Arrange potato skins on cookie sheet.
5. Brush insides of potato skins with butter and bake 8–12 minutes, or until golden and crispy. Remove from oven.
6. Sprinkle potato skins with cheese and bake for another 5 minutes, or until cheese melts.
7. Sprinkle crumbled bacon on top of each skin. Add a dollop of sour cream and top with olives and chives. Serve while hot.

Makes 16 skins.

SUPER NACHOS

1 16-ounce can refried beans
1 tablespoon taco seasoning
2 cups tomatoes, diced
2 tablespoons cilantro, minced
2 avocados
2 teaspoons lemon juice
1 8- to 10-ounce bag tortilla chips
$^1/_4$ lb. grated Monterey Jack cheese
$^1/_4$ lb. grated cheddar cheese
8 ounces sour cream
3 jalapeño peppers (optional), minced

1. Preheat oven to 400°F.
2. In a saucepan, mix refried beans and taco seasoning. Cook over medium heat until bubbly. Remove from heat.
3. In a small bowl, combine tomatoes and cilantro until well blended.
4. In a separate bowl, mash avocados with lemon juice until well blended.
5. Arrange chips evenly on a large cookie sheet or ovenproof platter. Spread a layer of refried beans on chips. Sprinkle grated cheese over beans. Spread tomatoes evenly on top. Bake 3–5 minutes, or until cheese is melted.

6. Spoon avocado mixture on top of nachos. Top with sour cream. Sprinkle with sliced chilies if desired. Eat immediately!

Makes 8 to 10 servings.

CHEESY PIZZA BREAD

2 (8-ounce) packages cream cheese, softened
$1^1/_4$ cups sour cream
1 cup shredded mozzarella cheese
$^1/_2$ cup shredded cheddar cheese
1 cup pizza sauce
$^2/_3$ cup chopped red bell pepper
$^1/_2$ cup sliced green onions
1 teaspoon dried oregano
$^1/_2$ teaspoon crushed red pepper flakes
$^1/_4$ teaspoon minced garlic
1 loaf crusty French bread

1. Preheat oven to 350°F.
2. In a medium baking dish, combine all the ingredients except bread.
3. Bake 5 minutes, or until bubbly and lightly browned. Remove from oven.
4. While sauce is cooling, place crusty bread in oven for 2 minutes—don't let it burn!
5. Spoon your warm pizza sauce onto bread and enjoy.

Makes 2 servings.

210

POPCORN TOPPERS

Toss one quart of popcorn with any of these fun flavors:

TEX-MEX POPCORN

1 teaspoon chili powder
1 teaspoon paprika
1 teaspoon cumin
2 tablespoons melted butter

CINNAMON POPCORN

1 tablespoon sugar
$1^1/_2$ teaspoons cinnamon
2 tablespoons melted butter

CHOCOLATE POPCORN

1/4 cup sugar
$1^1/_2$ teaspoons cocoa powder
$1^1/_2$ teaspoons butter
2 tablespoons evaporated milk
$1/_8$ teaspoon vanilla

Combine all ingredients in a saucepan and bring to a boil, stirring frequently. Pour over popcorn and toss.

ZESTY POPCORN

4 tablespoons grated Parmesan cheese
1 tablespoon Italian seasoning
4 teaspoons melted butter

CHEESY POPCORN

4 tablespoons grated sharp cheese
4 teaspoons melted butter
$1/_2$ teaspoon garlic salt

MEXICAN POPCORN

2 tablespoons melted butter
1 tablespoon taco seasoning

MUST-READ BOOKS

In addition to the favorite titles excerpted in this book, here are other well-loved stories to add to your reading list. Happy reading!

THE BOOK OF THREE by Lloyd Alexander

Taran, would-be hero and assistant pig keeper, assembles a group of companions to rescue the oracular pig Hen Wen from the forces of evil. One book in the five Prydian Chronicles.

THE CRICKET IN TIMES SQUARE by George Selden

A fast-talking mouse and a city-wise cat welcome a country cricket to a new home in a NYC subway station.

ENCYCLOPEDIA BROWN: BOY DETECTIVE by Donald Sobol

The first in a series of detective stories in which the reader is challenged to match wits with the 10-year-old mastermind of Idaville's war on crime.

HARRY POTTER AND THE SORCERER'S STONE by J. K. Rowling

The first book in a series of tales about a young wizard in training. From kids to adults, no one can get enough of Harry and his magical adventures.

THE HOBBIT by J. R. R. Tolkien

A completely normal, happy hobbit is not pleased when a wizard knocks on his front door looking for an adventurer, but this small upset turns into a grand quest with trolls, giant spiders, and magic rings.

HOW TO EAT FRIED WORMS by Thomas Rockwell

Would you eat fifteen worms in fifteen days for fifty dollars? Billy intends to do so in order to buy the minibike he's been dreaming of.

JAMES AND THE GIANT PEACH by Roald Dahl

After a terrible rhinoceros accident takes away his parents, poor James is forced to live with his horrible aunt and uncle until a bag of magic crystals changes his life.

MANIAC MAGEE by Jerry Spinelli

After his parents die, Jeffrey Lionel Magee's life becomes legendary, as he accomplishes athletic and other feats that hold his contemporaries in awe. 1991 Newbery Award.

TREASURE ISLAND by Robert Louis Stevenson

Some walk the plank, and some find buried treasure, while young Jim Hawkins tries to survive the infamous Long John Silver in this sweeping pirate epic.

MUST-READ BOOKS

WELCOME TO DEAD HOUSE, GOOSEBUMPS NO. 1 by R. L. Stine
In this first book of the popular Goosebumps series, two children are thrilled when their father inherits an old house-that is, until they realize that it's haunted.

THE WIND IN THE WILLOWS by Kenneth Grahame
Join Badger, Mole, Rat, and Toad as they struggle between the quiet, easy way of the River Bankers and the boisterous, excitable Wild Wooders.

Young Achievers

YOUNGEST ARTIST
Before most babies learn how to talk, Georgie Pocheptsov, not yet 2, was already drawing sketches. By 7, he was selling paintings at $11,000 apiece, and today, there is a twenty-month waiting period to buy them.

YOUNGEST SELF-MADE MILLIONAIRE
The child film actor Jackie Coogan, later famous for his role as Uncle Fester on *The Addams Family*, is the youngest male to have become a millionaire. From 1923 to 1924, Coogan earned $22,000 a week (over $220,000 in today's terms), retaining about 60 percent of his film's profits. By the age of 13, he had earned a million dollars.

YOUNGEST CHEF

Already nationally renowned for his culinary talent at the age of 5, Justin Miller published his own cookbook, *Cooking with Justin: Recipes for Kids (and Parents)*, at 7 years of age. Considered the world's youngest chef, 12-year old Justin is presently working on his second cookbook, *Break an Egg*, and he advises the Marriot Hotel chain on its children's menus.

YOUNGEST NO. 1 SOLO ARTIST

At 13 years, 3 months old, Stevie Wonder's album *Little Stevie Wonder– The Twelve Year Old Genius* (1963) topped U.S. sales charts.

YOUNGEST NO. 1 SOLO RAPPER

Born on March 9, 1987, Shad Gregory Moss of Columbus, OH, has been rapping since the age of 5. First appearing on stage when he was 6, he left an impression on multimillion-selling rap superstar, Snoop Doggy Dogg, who later dubbed him Lil' Bow Wow. According to the Recording Industry Association of America, his single "Bounce With Me" was the No. 1 Rap single for eight weeks, making him the No. 1 solo rapper on U.S. charts.

YOUNGEST SERIES WRITER

Young Lebanese writer Randy Nahle had his first book published in July 1998, when he was only 12 years old. After *Revenge*, he wrote the second book of his Hawk Archives detective series, *Mirror Image*, at the age of 13, which was published later in February 2000, when he was 14.

YOUNGEST GRADUATE

On June 5, 1994, Michael Kearney became the youngest college graduate on record when he earned a BA in anthropology from the University of South Alabama. He was 10 years, 4 months old.

Lemuel Gulliver is an average man of average intelligence. A gentle ship's surgeon, he serves as narrator of *Gulliver's Travels*. Over the course of the narrative, the unsophisticated storyteller makes four journeys to "remote nations of the world." Below are excerpts from his initial two voyages— among the most fantastic and memorable adventures in all of English literature. Gulliver first sets sail aboard the *Antelope*, and he and his shipmates encounter a deadly storm. Shipwrecked in Lilliput, Gulliver discovers the pocket-sized Lilliputians (one twelfth Gulliver's size) with their enormous egos. The next voyage, this time aboard the *Adventure*, sees Gulliver abandoned by the ship's crew at Brobdingnag, where the inhabitants are ten times his size! In *Gulliver's Travels*, Jonathan Swift (1667–1745) created an ingenious work of remarkable wit and texture. Upon publication in 1726, *Gulliver* was read by children for the inventive story and by adults for the political satire. More than 275 years later, the tale of imaginary voyages continues to draw a following for both its simplicity and multiple layers of meaning; its playfulness in the face of a grim vision of humanity; its marvelous fantasy worlds and the relative realism of its characters.

A Voyage to Lilliput

I lay down on the Grass, which was very short and soft, where I slept sounder than ever I remember to have done in my Life, and, as I reckoned, above Nine Hours; for when I awakened, it was just Daylight. I attempted to rise, but was not able to stir: For as I happen'd to lye on my Back, I found my Arms and Legs were strongly fastened on each Side to the Ground; and my Hair, which was long and thick, tied down in the same Manner. I likewise felt several slender Ligatures across my Body, from my Armpits to my Thighs. I could only look upwards; the Sun began to grow hot, and the Light offended my Eyes. I heard a confused Noise about me, but in the Posture I lay, could see nothing except the Sky. In a little time I felt something alive moving on my left Leg, which advancing gently forward over my Breast, came almost up to my Chin; when bending my Eyes downwards as much as I could, I perceived it to be a human Creature not six Inches high, with a Bow and Arrow in his hands, and a Quiver at his Back. In the meantime, I felt at least Forty more of the same Kind (as I conjectured) following the first. I was in the utmost Astonishment, and roared so loud, that they all ran back in a Fright; and some of them, as I was afterwards told, were hurt with the Falls they got by leaping from my Sides upon the Ground. However, they soon returned, and one of them, who ventured so far as to get a full Sight of my Face,

Gulliver's Travels
by Jonathan Swift

lifting up his Hands and Eyes by way of Admiration, cried out in a shrill but distinct Voice, *Hekinah Degul*: the others repeated the same Words several times, but I then knew not what they meant. I lay all this while, as the Reader may believe, in great Uneasiness; At length, struggling to get loose, I had the Fortune to break the Strings, and wrench out the Pegs that fastened my left Arm to the Ground; for, by lifting it up to my Face, I discovered the Methods they had taken to bind me, and at the same time, with a violent Pull, which gave me excessive Pain, I a little loosened the Strings that tied down my Hair on the left Side, so that I was just able to turn my Head about two Inches. But the creatures ran off a second time, before I could seize them; Whereupon there was a great Shout in a very shrill Accent, and after it ceased, I heard one of them cry aloud, *Tolgo Phonac*; when in an Instant I felt above a Hundred Arrows discharged on my left Hand, which pricked me like so many Needles; and besides they shot another Flight into the Air, as we do Bombs in Europe, whereof many, I suppose, fell on my Body (though I felt them not) and some on my Face, which I immediately covered with my left

Hand. When this Shower of Arrows was over, I fell a groaning with Grief and Pain, and then striving again to get loose, they discharged another Volly larger than the first, and some of them attempted with Spears to stick me in the Sides; but, by good Luck, I had on me a Buff Jerkin, which they could not pierce. I thought it the most prudent Method to lie still, and my Design was to continue so till Night, when, my left Hand being already loose, I could easily free myself: And as for the Inhabitants, I had Reason to believe I might be a Match for the greatest Armies they could bring against me, if they were all of the same Size with him that I saw.

I perceived it to be a human Creature not six Inches high, with a Bow and Arrow in his hands, . . .

A VOYAGE TO BROBDINGNAG

One of the Reapers approaching within ten Yards of the Ridge where I lay, made me apprehend that with the next Step I should be squashed to Death under his Foot, or cut in two with his Reaping hook. And therefore when he was again about to move, I screamed as loud as Fear could make me. Whereupon the huge Creature trod short, and looking round about under him for some time, at last espied me as I lay on the Ground. He considered a while with the Caution of one who endeavours to lay hold on a small dangerous Animal in such a Manner that it shall not be able either to scratch or to bite him, as I myself have sometimes done with a Weasel in England. At length he ventured to take me up behind by the

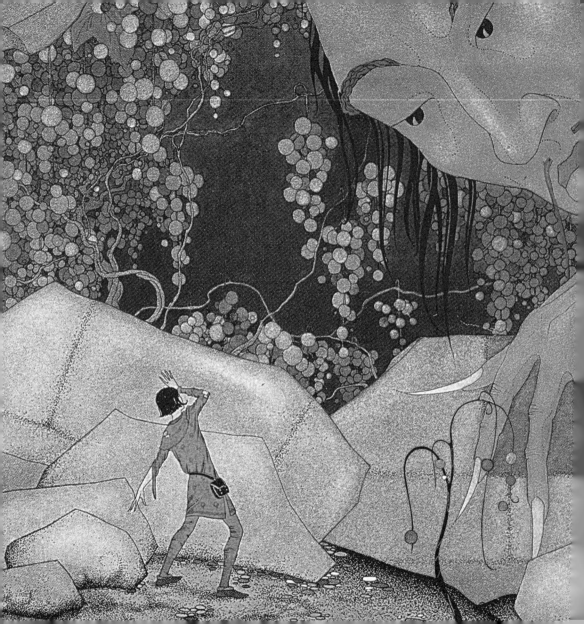

Middle between his fore Finger and Thumb, and brought me within three Yards of his Eyes, that he might behold my Shape more perfectly. I guessed his Meaning, and my good Fortune gave me so much Presence of Mind, that I resolved not to struggle in the least as he held me in the Air, about sixty Foot from the Ground, although he grievously pinched my Sides, for fear I should slip through his Fingers. All I ventured was to raise my Eyes towards the Sun, and place my Hands together in a supplicating Posture, and to speak some Words in an humble melancholy Tone, suitable to the Condition I then was in. For I apprehended every moment that he would dash me against the Ground, as we usually do any little hateful Animal which we have a mind to destroy. But my good Star would have it, that he

At length he ventured to take me up behind by the Middle between his fore Finger and Thumb, ...

appeared pleased with my Voice and Gestures, and began to look upon me as a Curiosity, much wondering to hear me pronounce articulate Words, although he could not understand them. In the mean time I was not able to forbear groaning and shedding Tears, and turning my Head towards my Sides; letting him know, as well as I could, how cruelly I was hurt by the Pressure of his Thumb and Finger. He seemed to apprehend my Meaning; for, lifting up the Lappet of his Coat, he put me gently into it, and immediately ran along with me to his Master, who was a substantial Farmer, and the same Person I had first seen in the Field.

It was
a time
when
reptiles
were
king.

The "terrible lizards" once reigned over the Earth, but today we have only their bones as evidence that they existed. They ranged in all different shapes and sizes, from the behemoth brachiosaurus to the chicken-like compsognathus. Some had teeth the size of saws, and others may even have had feathers! Whatever else their fossils tell us, though, one thing is certain: It was a time when reptiles were king.

APATOSAURUS (a.k.a. *Brontosaurus*) Apatosaurus was a gentle giant. Measuring up to 90 feet long and weighing 70,000 pounds, with a tiny brain and a whip-like tail, apatosaurus left footprints a yard wide. He had to have grazed constantly to fill his enormous body. Apatosaurus lived during the late Jurassic period.

DINOSAURS

ARCHAEOPTERYX

Archaeopteryx was the world's earliest known bird. Not much bigger than a grown-up's hand, archaeopteryx lived in the late Jurassic period and was related to the dinosaurs—in fact, archaeopteryx was a lot like a reptile, only it had feathers!

BRACHIOSAURUS

At 120,000 pounds, Brachiosaurus was the heaviest creature that ever walked the earth. Brachiosaurus got its name, meaning "arm lizard," from its unusually long forelegs. Its head towered 50 feet above the ground and each of its neck vertebrae was 3 feet long! Brachiosaurus was a plant eater and lived during the late Jurassic period.

COMPSOGNATHUS

Compsognathus was the smallest dinosaur. At 3 feet long and about 6.5 pounds, he was only a little bit bigger than a chicken. This meat eater, whose name means "pretty jaw," walked on his hind legs and had two claws on each of his forelegs. Compsognathus lived during the late Jurassic period in what is now western Europe.

When Dinosaurs Lived

All the dinosaurs lived during the Mesozoic Era, which lasted from 248 million years ago until the great extinction, which happened 65 million years ago. The Mesozoic is divided into three periods:

The TRIASSIC (245 to 208 million years ago), when most of the dinosaurs' smaller ancestors lived on one great land mass.

The JURASSIC (208 to 144 million years ago), when dinosaurs developed and grew enormous, and the land split into two continents.

The CRETACEOUS (144 to 65 million years ago), when the continents split up further, and dinosaur species became separated.

DINOSAURS

PTERODACTYL
(*Pterosaur*)

Meaning "wing finger," ptero-dactylus (one of the smallest of the pterosaurs) was a flying reptile who lived during the Cretaceous peri-od. With hollow bones and leathery wings that spanned three feet, pterodacty-lus was a small but fierce dinosaur. His ability to fly made him a terror to creatures of the sea, which were his favorite lunch.

STEGOSAURUS

Though stegosaurus could be 30 feet long and weigh nearly 7,000 pounds, his brain was only the size of a walnut! He was a gentle herbivore from the late Jurassic period whose plates sticking up from his spine made him stand out from the crowd. He defended him-self with the 4-foot-long spikes at the end of his tail.

TRICERATOPS

Triceratops is named for the three horns on his face—horns that could be up to 3 feet long, coming out of a face and neck frill that could be 7 feet wide! These plant eaters from the late Cretaceous period were a tough bunch—many skeletons show wounds from fights.

DINOSAURS

TYRANNOSAURUS REX
Everyone's favorite monster, Tyrannosaurus rex's name means "king of the tyrant reptiles." Rex lived during the late Cretaceous period and was the biggest carnivorous dinosaur to live in any era. He was about 15 feet tall and 40 feet long, and weighed 12,000 pounds. His teeth, 6 inches long and serrated, were not to be argued with!

ULTRASAURUS (*Supersaurus*)
Ultrasaurus is a mystery dinosaur—only the bones of one leg have been found. But if scientists are correct about the leg's clues, ultrasaurus could be the biggest land animal ever (its leg bones are a third larger than brachiosaurus's)! Ultrasaurus roamed what is now North America in the early Cretaceous period.

VELOCIRAPTOR
The velociraptor, whose name means "speedy predator," was about 6 feet from teeth to tail. One nearly complete velociraptor skeleton has survived all those years since the Cretaceous period—and it was found curled in an attack position, holding tight to the skeleton of another dinosaur. A true fight to the death!

Puff the Magic Dragon

by Peter Yarrow and
Lenny Lipton

Oh! Puff the Magic Dragon
lived by the sea
And frolicked in the
autumn mist in a land
called Honalee.

Puff the Magic Dragon lived by the sea
And frolicked in the autumn mist in a land called Honalee.
Little Jackie Paper loved that rascal Puff
And brought him strings and sealing wax and other fancy stuff.

(Chorus)

Together they would travel on a boat with billowed sail.
Jackie kept a lookout perched on Puff's gigantic tail.
Noble kings and princes would bow whene'er they came.
Pirate ships would low'r their flag when Puff
    roared out his name.

(Chorus)

A dragon lives forever, but not so little boys.
Painted wings and giant rings make way for other toys.
One gray night it happened, Jackie Paper came no more,
And Puff that mighty dragon, he ceased his fearless roar.

(Chorus)

His head was bent in sorrow, green tears fell like rain.
Puff no longer went to play along the Cherry Lane.
Without his lifelong friend, Puff could not be brave,
So Puff that mighty dragon sadly slipped into his cave.

(Chorus)

Dreams by Langston Hughes

Hold fast to *dreams*
For if dreams die
Life is a broken-winged bird
That cannot fly.

Hold fast to *dreams*
For when dreams go
Life is a barren field
Frozen with snow.

STAR GAZERS

The night sky looks different in Gnome, Alaska, from the way it looks in Miami, Florida. And the stars will be in a different place in the summer night skies from where they are in the winter, spring, or fall. You may know how to spot the Big Dipper and Orion's Belt, but do you know how to find Pegasus, the flying horse, or Draco the dragon? Here's an easy way to make your own star chart. Then you can try to map out constellations as they appear from your backyard.

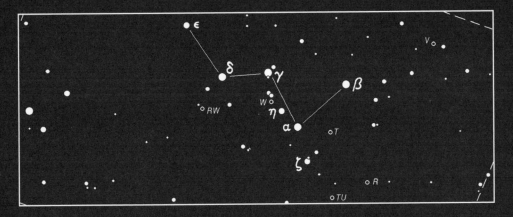

Star chart, aluminum foil, straight pins, 2-liter plastic soda bottle, scissors, black construction paper, tape, penlight

1. Place the star chart over the shiny side of a piece of aluminum foil. With a straight pin, poke a tiny hole through each major star so that the pin goes through the foil. When you're done, the foil should be a replica of the major stars in your star chart.

2. Ask an adult to help you cut the bottom off the soda bottle. Wrap the bottle in construction paper and tape it in place.

3. Cover the bottom of the soda bottle with the aluminum foil. Make sure that the shiny side of the foil faces the inside of the bottle. Tape the foil in place.

4. Look through the mouth of the bottle. The pinpricks of light should be a good representation of the night sky. Try shining a penlight through the mouth of the bottle in a dark room and casting your stars against the wall. You can use your star map to identify the constellations. Then on the next clear night, go outside and try out your star gazer bottle to help find the real constellations.

Questions

Why is the sky blue?

Light travels in waves, and the distance between the crests of two waves is called the wavelength. Blue light has a shorter wavelength than most other colors, and when it hits our atmosphere, the nitrogen and oxygen molecules in the air scatter blue light ten times more than other visible colors. We see different colors at sunset because the sun, now low on the horizon, scatters the blue light out of our line of vision.

Why is the ocean blue?

Because it reflects the sky.

Why are clouds white?

Clouds are made up of tiny particles of water and ice that reflect all color wavelengths equally. Since all colors of light seen together appear as white light, white becomes the color of clouds.

What is the greenhouse effect?

The greenhouse effect occurs as radiation from the sun passes into our atmosphere and gets trapped. "Greenhouse" gases (like water vapor, carbon dioxide, methane, and others) keep the radiation (warmth) from passing back out again. This isn't a bad thing, as it keeps the atmosphere warm enough for us to live. However, human activity has been creating an unnaturally large amount of greenhouse gases, trapping too much heat. The greenhouse effect causes global warming, and *that's* definitely not a good thing.

What is acid rain?

Acid rain refers to the way acids fall out of the atmosphere. When acidic elements in certain gases combine with water and oxygen to form acidic compounds, acids can come down in the rain. Acid also forms dry particles which are blown onto trees, buildings, and so on. When it rains, these "dry" acids mix with the rainwater. Acid rain causes damage to forests, soils, marine life, and human health.

What causes acid rain?

The majority of these acidic gases, like sulfur dioxide and nitrogen oxides, are released into the atmosphere by burning fossil fuels, like coal, to make electric power. We can reduce the level of acidity in rainwater by conserving electricity.

What's the moon really made of?

Approximately half of our moon's surface, called lowlands, or *maria*, is made up of areas of volcanic rock that's a lot like that found on Earth. This kind of rock is called *basalt*, and is formed when volcanoes erupt, spewing out molten material that then cools. Basalt is rich in iron and magnesium. The second main type of rock, *breccia*, is made of soil and pieces of rock squashed together by meteorites.

The far side of the moon's surface is made up mostly of mountainous areas called *bright highlands*. These mountains have huge craters.

Why do stars appear to have points?

When we look at stars through a lens (including the lenses in our eyes), the light they give off is diffracted and shoots off in all directions.

What's the difference between a comet and a shooting star?

Comets are big balls of ice and dust hurtling through space. When comets pass near the sun, the ice melts and becomes gas—that's the tail. Unless it collides with something, a comet never dies.

Shooting stars (meteors) are chunks of sand or ice that have hit the Earth's atmosphere. When they do, they immediately burn up, producing the fiery effect of a star. Meteor showers happen when the Earth passes through a comet's orbit: Scattered along the orbit are bits of debris that enter the Earth's atmosphere as the Earth moves through the orbit.

Will we ever put a person on Mars?

Maybe, maybe not. It could take up to a year just to get there, and we still don't know how to keep an astronaut healthy in space for that long (he body is designed to live with gravity, and doesn't do so well without it). Once the astronauts arrived, how would they breathe? What would they eat? How would they stay warm enough, being so far from the sun? Once we figure out the answers to these questions, it's only a matter of time before those dreams become reality!

What is a black hole?

When large stars die, they don't just fade away—they go out with a bang! This bang is called a *supernova*. In some cases, the material that's left becomes infinitely dense, and the gravitational pull of this mass is so strong, not even light can escape it!

What is the big bang theory?

The big bang theory is the most popular explanation for how the universe began. It says that all the matter in the universe used to be condensed into one point. Sometime between 10 and 20 billion years ago, the tiny point exploded, sending matter off in all directions. As everything cooled down, separate bodies were formed—the planets and the stars.

What is an asteroid made of?

Iron or stone. There are believed to be millions of them in space.

How many stars are there in the universe?

We know that our galaxy, the Milky Way, is home to hundreds of billions of stars. If there are 100 billion stars in each of the 50 billion galaxies in the universe, the number of stars would be 5,000,000,000,000,000,000,000,000,000,000—or five octillion!

What is the Earth made of?

From the core to the crust, the Earth is 34.6% Iron, 29.5% Oxygen , 15.2% Silicon, 12.7% Magnesium, 2.4% Nickel,

Our World, Our Universe

1.9% Sulfur, 0.05% Titanium.

How fast does the Earth orbit the sun?
At 67,000 miles per hour, or 18.6 miles per second.

How fast does the moon orbit the Earth?
At approximately 23,000 miles per hour.

How old is the Earth?
The Earth was created approximately 4,500 million years ago. The universe began approximately 15,000 million years ago.

What causes waves?
The wind. The longer the distance the wind has traveled, the more pressure it exerts on the ocean. The stronger the wind, the larger the waves. After the waves lift, gravity brings them back down again.

Waves of water only move up and down. They cannot move horizontally.

How old are the seas?
Scientists believe our seas are as much as 500 million years old.

What is Glaciology?
The study of icebergs.

How hot is the sun?
The surface of the sun burns at about 11,000°F. The core of the sun burns over 20,000,000°F.

Is the sun a star?
Yes, it is. The reason you can see the sun as opposed to the other billions and billions of stars is because it is only 8 light-minutes away from the Earth. Most stars are thousands and thousands of light-years away.

What is the hardest substance in the world?
Diamonds are the world's hardest natural substance. They are produced in extreme heat deep within the Earth's crust over billions of years.

The next time you're in the mood for something sweet, whip up one of these easy and mouth-watering beverages.

BANANA BAVARIA SHAKE

1 cups milk
2 ripe bananas
2 scoops chocolate ice cream

Combine all ingredients in a blender and mix until smooth.

Makes 2 servings.

PURPLE COW

1 12-ounce can frozen grape juice
3 cups milk

Place ingredients in a blender and mix until smooth and frothy.

Makes 4 servings.

ROOT BEER FLOAT

24 ounces (2 cans) root beer
4 scoops vanilla ice cream or frozen yogurt

1. Pour root beer evenly into four tall glasses.
2. Drop a scoop of ice cream or frozen yogurt into each glass. The ice cream will fizz and develop an icy crust.

3. Serve with sundae spoons and straws and slurp immediately!

Makes 4 servings.

PEANUT À LA MOO

$1/2$ cup chunky peanut butter
2 cups milk
4 scoops vanilla ice cream

Put all ingredients in a blender. Pulse a few times until consistency is frothy. Be careful not to overblend. Pour in sundae glasses and serve with a straw.

Makes 4 servings.

CITRUS GINGER FIZZ

$1/2$ cup lemon juice
$1/4$ cup lime juice
1 teaspoon powdered sugar
1 tablespoon sugar
16 ounces seltzer
4 lime slices

1. In a large pitcher, combine lemon juice, lime juice, powdered sugar, and sugar. Stir with a wooden spoon until blended.
2. Add seltzer and stir again.
3. Pour into tall glasses over ice cubes and serve with lime slices.

Makes 4 servings.

Pinhole Camera

The word photography *comes from the Greek term meaning "light writing." In ancient times, people learned that light passing through a pinhole would cast images into a dark room. The word* camera *comes from the Latin word for "room." By the 1700s, people discovered that certain chemical combinations turned dark when exposed to sunlight. Soon, they would learn to combine the use of cameras and chemically treated plates to make photographs. By making your own pinhole camera, you will have a chance to see up close (and upside down!) how images can be "written" in light. Then, on the next sunny day, see what develops!*

Marker, cylindrical potato-chip can or tennis-ball can with clear plastic lid, utility knife, duct tape, aluminum foil, pushpin

1. Carefully draw a circle around the circumference of the can about two inches from the bottom.
2. Ask an adult to cut your can in two pieces along the line. The edges should be smooth and even.
3. Remove the plastic lid from the top of the can and cover the newly cut shorter portion.
4. Tape the can back together with duct tape. Try to make the two segments fit as snugly as possible.
5. To avoid getting any light in your pinhole camera, cover the entire can in duct tape.
6. With the pushpin, carefully poke a pinhole in the center of the bottom of the can.
7. Go to a well-lit or sunny area and look in the open end of the can. You may need to cup your hand around your eye to prevent additional light from getting inside the tube. Light that enters through the pinhole will project an upside down image on the plastic lid inside the tube. Now you've got an eye for photography!

Alexander (Alec) Ramsay is passionate about horses. Homeward bound following his two-month trip to India to visit his missionary uncle, Alec is at once electrified and crestfallen. While Alec was in India, his uncle had taught him how to be a skilled horseman. Yet he knew that opportunities to ride back home in New York City would be few and far between. When the steamer *Drake* stops to board a beautiful but fierce stallion, "a stallion with a wonderful physical perfection that matched his savage, ruthless spirit," the long trip home becomes an adventure. Disaster strikes when a great storm shipwrecks the *Drake* off the Spanish coast. Alec and the Black are stranded on a barren island, and must learn to rely on each other for survival. The Black both terrorizes and mesmerizes Alec, whose greatest desire is to ride the stallion and make him his trusted friend. Walter Farley began writing *The Black Stallion* (1941) while he was a high school student in Brooklyn, New York. He went on to pen twenty more books featuring the Black—now the most famous horse in all of literature. Farley's books—not one of which has ever gone out of print—have been translated into more than twenty languages.

Days passed and gradually the friendship between the boy and the Black grew. The stallion now came at his call and let Alec stroke him while he grazed. One night Alec sat within the warm glow of the fire and watched the stallion munching on the carragheen beside the pool. He wondered if the stallion was as tired of the carragheen as he. Alec had found that if he boiled it in the turtle shell it formed a gelatinous substance which tasted a little better than the raw moss. A fish was now a rare delicacy to him.

The flame's shadows reached out and cast eerie ghost-like patterns on the Black's body. Alec's face became grim as thoughts rushed through his brain. Should he try it tomorrow? Did he dare attempt to ride the Black? Should he wait a few more days? Go ahead—tomorrow. *Don't do it!* Go ahead—

The fire burned low, then smoldered. Yet Alec sat beside the fire, his eyes fixed on that blacker-than-night figure beside the spring.

The next morning he woke from a fitful slumber to find the sun high above. Hurriedly he ate some of the carragheen. Then he looked for the Black, but he was not in sight. Alec whistled, but no answer came. He walked toward the hill. The sun blazed down and

The
Black
Stallion

by
Walter Farley

247

the sweat ran from his body. If is would only rain! The last week had been like an oven on the island.

When he reached the top of the hill, he saw the Black at one end of the beach. Again he whistled, and this time there was an answering whistle as the stallion turned his head. Alec walked up the beach toward him.

The Black stood still as he approached. He went cautiously up to him and placed a hand on his neck. "Steady," he murmured, as the warm skin quivered slightly beneath his hand. The stallion showed neither fear nor hate of him; his large eyes were still turned toward the sea.

For a moment Alec stood with his hand on the Black's neck. Then he walked toward a sand dune a short distance away. The stallion followed. He stepped up the side of the dune, his left hand in the horse's thick mane. The Black's ears pricked forward, his eyes followed the boy nervously—some of the savageness returned to them, his muscles twitched. For a moment Alec was undecided what to do. Then his hands gripped the mane tighter and he threw himself on the Black's back. For a second the stallion stood motionless, then he snorted and plunged; the sand went flying as he doubled in the air. Alec felt the mighty muscles heave, then he was flung through the air, landing heavily on his back. Everything went dark.

Alec regained consciousness to find something warm against his cheek. Slowly he opened his eyes. The stallion was pushing him with his

"Steady," he murmured, as the warm skin quivered slightly beneath his hand.

head. Alec tried moving his arms and legs, and found them bruised but not broken. Warily he got to his feet. The wildness and savageness had once more disappeared in the Black; he looked as though nothing had happened.

Alec waited for a few minutes—then once again led the stallion to the sand dune. His hand grasped the horse's mane. But this time he laid only the upper part of his body on the stallion's back, while he talked soothingly into his ear. The Black flirted his ears back and forth, as he glanced backward with his dark eyes.

"See, I'm not going to hurt you," Alec murmured, knowing it was he who might be hurt. After a few minutes, Alec cautiously slid onto his back. Once again, the stallion snorted and sent the boy flying through the air.

Alec picked himself up from the ground—slower this time. But when he had rested, he whistled for the Black again. The stallion moved toward him. Alec determinedly stepped on the sand dune and once again let the Black feel his weight. Gently he spoke into a large ear, "It's me. I'm not much to carry." He slid onto the stallion's back. One arm slipped around the Black's neck as he half-reared. Then like a shot from a gun, the Black broke down the beach. His action shifted, and his huge strides seemed to make him fly through the air.

Alec clung to the stallion's mane for his life. The wind screamed by and he couldn't see! Suddenly the Black swerved and headed up the sand dune; he reached the top and then down. The spring was a blur as they whipped by. To the rocks he raced, and then the stallion made a wide circle—his speed never diminishing. Down through a long ravine he rushed. Alec's blurred vision made out a black object in front of them, and as a flash he remembered the deep gully that was there. He felt the stallion gather himself; instinctively he leaned forward and held the Black firm and steady with his hands and knees. Then they were in the air, sailing over the black hold. Alec almost lost his balance when they landed but recovered himself in time to keep from falling off! Once again the stallion reached the beach, his hoofbeats regular and rhythmic on the white sand.

The jump had helped greatly in clearing Alec's mind. He leaned closer to the stallion's ear and kept repeating, "Easy, Black. Easy." The stallion seemed to glide over the sand and then his speed began to lessen. Alec kept talking to him. Slower and slower ran the Black. Gradually he came to a stop. The boy released his grip from the stallion's mane and his arms encircled the Black's neck. He was weak with exhaustion—in no condition for such a ride!

Wearily he slipped to the ground. Never had he dreamed a horse could run so fast!

Wearily he slipped to the ground. Never had he dreamed a horse could run so fast! The stallion looked at him, his head held high, his large body only slightly covered with sweat.

That night Alec lay wide awake, his body aching with pain, but his heart pounding with excitement. He had ridden the Black! He had conquered this wild, unbroken stallion with kindness. He felt sure that from that day on the Black was his—his alone! But for what—would they ever be rescued? Would he ever see his home again? Alec shook his head. He had promised himself he wouldn't think of that any more.

Well, son, I'll tell you:
Life for me ain't been no crystal stair.
It's had tacks in it,
And splinters,
And boards torn up,
And places with no carpet on the floor—
Bare.
But all the time
I'se been a-climbin' on,
And reachin' landin's,
And turnin' corners,
And sometimes goin' in the dark
Where there ain't been no light.
So, boy, don't you turn back.
Don't you set down on the steps
'Cause you finds it kinder hard.
Don't you fall now—
For I'se still goin', honey,
I'se still climbin',
And life for me ain't been no crystal stair.

Mother To Son

by Langston Hughes

Questions

1 Which monster can you fend off with garlic?

   A. Frankenstein

   B. Wolfman

   C. Count Dracula

   D. Your sister

   E. The Loch Ness Monster

2 Which of these countries is the Panda from?

   A. Zambia

   B. United States

   C. China

   D. Singapore

   E. France

3 What is the name of Harry Potter's favorite sport?

   A. Fufulopp

   B. Didditch

   C. Cricket

   D. Quidditch

   E. Table tennis

4 Which of these superheroes is THE MAN OF STEEL?

   A. Batman

   B. Spiderman

   C. Superman

   D. Iron Man

   E. The Flash

5 Which set of numbers is in the correct sequence?

   A. 1, 2, 5, 3, 4

   B. 38, 37, 36, 30, 35

   C. 105, 107, 108, 117

   D. 12, 14, 16, 18, 20

   E. -9, -7, 5, -3

6 What is the largest state in the United States of America?

   A. Nevada

   B. Montana

   C. California

   D. Texas

   E. Alaska

& Answers

Test Yourself!

7 Horses rely heavily on _____ to communicate with people as well as other horses.

- A. E-mail
- B. Sound
- C. Touch
- D. Smell
- E. Telephones

8 What causes earthquakes?

- A. Small trolls digging inside the center of the Earth
- B. Energy that causes the Earth's plates to scrape against each other
- C. Intense heat in the center of the Earth
- D. An eclipse of the moon
- E. An explosion on the outer surface of the Earth

9 Which of these baseball players scored the most home runs in his career?

- A. Babe Ruth
- B. Willie Mays
- C. Hank Aaron
- D. Reggie Jackson
- E. Mickey Mantle

10 Who invented the telephone?

- A. Alexander Jacob Bell
- B. Hermann von Hemholz
- C. Alexander Graham Bell
- D. Alexander von Telephone
- E. Samuel Morse

ANSWERS: 1: C; 2: C; 3: D; 4: C; 5: D; 6: E; 7: C; 8: B; 9: C; 10: C.

Light-Bulb Telegraph

Dit-dit-dit, dah-dah-dah, dit-dit-dit. You may recognize that as international Morse code for SOS. But you don't have to be a captain, a pilot, or a secret agent to send codes to your friends. You can make a telegraph by creating a simple electrical circuit, and be flashing messages in no time!

Telephone wire, wire stripper, block of wood or strip of cardboard, masking tape, 5 metal paper clips, flashlight bulb, D-cell battery, bulb holder (optional: available at hardware stores)

1. Start by cutting three lengths of wire. Strip an inch of the plastic insulation from each of the ends.
2. Use wood or cardboard to make the base for your telegraph. Secure the light bulb onto the base with masking tape. Spread open two paper clips. Take two wires and wrap an end of each around the inner fold of each clip. Wrap both clips around the base of the light bulb. Make sure the clips are contacting the metal base. Tape clips in place.
3. Wrap one end of the wires around a paper clip and tape to the negative (flat) end of the battery. Tape the battery in place onto your telegraph base.
4. Wrap the end of the other wire

(connected to the bulb) around a thumbtack, under the head, and press into the telegraph base to secure.

5. Take the remaining piece of wire and wrap each end around a paper clip. Attach one clip to the positive (knobby) end of the battery and secure it in place with tape. Touch the other paper clip to the thumbtack. This completes the circuit and lights the bulb. (If your bulb doesn't light up, check your connections!) Secure the paper clip to the base with another thumbtack.

6. To make a circuit breaker, bend the paper clip slightly apart so that it no longer touches the thumbtack connected to the light-bulb wire. Then, simply tap the clip to the thumbtack to complete the circuit and start sending secret messages!

Morse Code

Tap and release quickly to make a dot. Tap, hold, and release to make a dash.

A . −	I . .	Q − − . −	Y − . − −	7 − − . . .
B − . . .	J . − − −	R . − .	Z − − . .	8 − − − . .
C − . − .	K − . −	S . . .	1 . − − − −	9 − − − − .
D − . .	L . − . .	T −	2 . . − − −	0 − − − − −
E .	M − −	U . . −	3 . . . − −	, (comma) − − . − −
F . . − .	N − .	V . . . −	4 . . . . −	. (period) . − . − . −
G − − .	O − − −	W . − −	5	? . . − − . .
H	P . − − .	X − . . −	6 −	

MUST-SEE MOVIES!

THE 5,000 FINGERS OF DR. T (1953) stars Hans Conried, Tommy Rettig. Bart uncovers Dr. Terwilliker's crazy plan to force five hundred boys to practice at his gigantic piano twenty-four hours a day, seven days a week, in this live-action Dr. Seuss story.

A CHRISTMAS STORY (1983) stars Melinda Dillon, Darren McGavin, Peter Billingsley. A boy's only Christmas wish is for a Red Ryder BB gun in this hilarious story about the fun and craziness of Christmas in 1940s America.

THE ADVENTURES OF ROBIN HOOD (1938) stars Errol Flynn, Basil Rathbone, Olivia de Havilland. The first great action-adventure movie pits the courageous Robin and his Merry Men against the evil Prince John and Guy of Gisbourne.

BACK TO THE FUTURE (1985) stars Michael J. Fox, Christopher Lloyd. Eighties teenager Marty McFly travels back in time to the 1950s in order to save Doc Brown's life, but ends up causing more trouble when he stops his parents from meeting. Unless Marty can get his parents to fall in love, he becomes in danger of being erased from all time in this special-effects masterpiece.

CITY LIGHTS (1931) stars Charlie Chaplin. In this silent comedy, a tramp helps a beautiful poor blind girl he has fallen in love with. The boxing match in this film is one of Chaplin's funniest scenes.

DUCK SOUP (1933) stars the Marx Brothers. Crazy Groucho becomes president of the bankrupt country Freedonia and ends up starting a war with neighboring

Sylvania over the hand of Mrs. Teasdale. Harpo and Chico only add to the rising insanity in this satire of war, politics, and basically everything.

E. T.: THE EXTRA TERRESTRIAL (1982) stars Henry Thomas, Drew Barrymore. A group of children must protect a space alien from being captured, and send him back to his home planet.

JURASSIC PARK (1993) stars Sam Neil, Jeff Goldblum, Laura Dern, Richard Attenborough. Watch out, here comes the velociraptor! Millionaire Richard Attenborough asks two paleontologists and a mathematician to advise him on his cloned dinosaur theme park. Unfortunately, the dinosaurs escape! Amazing special affects and hair-raising suspense make this Steven Spielberg blockbuster one to watch.

THE KARATE KID (1984) stars Ralph Macchio, Pat Morita. Mr. Miyagi teaches Daniel-san martial arts when the boy moves to his neighborhood. Daniel learns the power of friendship and gains confidence as he overcomes school bullies and enters a karate competition.

KING KONG (1933) stars Fay Wray. A film crew discovers a gigantic ape on Skull island. Unfortunately, the ape falls in love with the film's female star. When the captured Kong is brought back to New York, the love-crazed monkey goes ape in the Big Apple. A true film classic with amazing stop-motion animation.

THE NEVERENDING STORY (1984) stars Barret Oliver. A young boy finds a magical book about a fantastic world in great danger. He learns to believe in himself and his own powerful imagination in his effort to save it.

PEE-WEE'S BIG ADVENTURE (1985) stars Paul Reubens. The very strange Pee-wee goes on a cross-country journey to recover his precious stolen bike. Along the way, he encounters ghosts, movie stars, convicts, and other hilarious characters.

MUST-SEE MOVIES!

THE PRINCESS BRIDE (1987) stars Cary Elwes, Robin Wright, Billy Crystal. A funny fairy-tale story, with some quirky twists, about a beautiful princess and her brave hero, with some giants, miracle men, and an evil prince thrown in.

STAGECOACH (1939) stars John Wayne. This is the quintessential Western movie, with plenty of action, gunfights, and savage Indians. The Ringo Kid must protect the fragile stagecoach passengers as they make their way across the American West.

STAR WARS (1977) A true sci-fi gem! The Jedi knight Ben (Obi-Wan) Kenobi enlists the help of the young Luke Skywalker, the roguish Han Solo, and the very hairy Chewbacca to restore the beautiful Princess Leia to her throne and to destroy the Death Star. The one that started it all.

WALLACE & GROMIT: THE WRONG TROUSERS (1993) An evil penguin uses Wallace and his fantastic mechanical trousers invention to commit a robbery. Its up to Gromit, Wallace's faithful dog, to save the day in this amazing animated short.

WHITE FANG (1991) stars Ethan Hawke. Jack London's famous adventure story about the friendship between a boy and a wolf-dog takes place during the exciting Yukon gold rush in the early 1900s.

WILLY WONKA AND THE CHOCOLATE FACTORY (1971) stars Gene Wilder. Charlie wins a chance to tour the tastiest factory in the world in this wonderful musical based on Roald Dahl's book.

THE WIZARD OF OZ (1939) stars Judy Garland. The classic story has Dorothy Gale on the road to Emerald City, looking for the Wizard of Oz in order to get back to her home in Kansas. Along the way, she meets the Scarecrow, the Lion, and the Tin Man, and battles the Wicked Witch of the West.

Additional favorites: *Superman; Old Yeller: Bringing Up Baby; Rookie of the Year*

One...Two... Three...Juggle!

Learn how to dazzle your friends with a trick that's been around for centuries! Whether you're entertaining kings and queens or kids and teens, you'll have as much fun showing off your new talent as your audience will have watching you. Once you get the hang of it, you'll be able to toss around all kinds of objects—just make sure they're not breakable!

Three balls, apples, or beanbags

1. Start with one ball. Toss it gently back and forth from one hand to the other. Try and make the ball arc at about eye level. Practice several times until your tosses are smooth and consistent. Tip: When you throw from right to left, try to make the ball arc in front of your left ear. When you throw from left to right, try to make the ball arc in front of your right ear.

2. Get ready for two balls! Have one ball in each hand. Using your right hand, toss the first ball in the air. When it reaches the highest point of its arc, toss the second ball (from your left hand to your right). When the second ball starts to arc, catch the first ball (with your left hand). Hold it. Then catch the second ball (with your right hand). Hold it. The trick is to make sure the balls don't hit each other in the air. Now try again, starting this time with your left hand instead of your right. Continue to practice until you can do several tosses in a row without dropping the balls.

3. Now for the tricky part: the third ball. Start by holding two balls in your right hand and one in your left. Toss the first ball in your right hand toward the left. When the ball arcs, toss the ball in your left hand toward the right. Catch the first ball in your left hand. As the second ball arcs, throw the last ball with your right hand toward your left. Catch the second ball with your right hand. Then catch the last ball in your left hand. Try it again starting with two balls in your left hand. Once you get the hang of it, see how many times in a row you can do it without dropping any balls.

"Whosoever pulleth out this sword of this stone and anvil, is rightwise King born of all England." So reads the inscription on the sword in the stone. The people of England take these words seriously, as there is no heir to the throne. The first in a series of four books that make up *The Once and Future King, The Sword in the Stone* (1938) relates the story of King Arthur's boyhood. Arthur, called "the Wart" in his youth, is the adopted son of Sir Ector, whose "proper" son is Kay. Young Arthur, who struggles both to become a man and to be considered an equal of his older brother, finds a wonderful tutor in the magician Merlyn. The wise magician instructs his pupil in unorthodox and imaginative ways, teaching Arthur that experience is the best learning tool in life. Terence Hanbury White (1906-1964) wrote the other books of the series over twenty years: *The Queen of Air and Darkness* (1939), *The Ill-Made Knight* (1940), and *The Candle in the Wind* (1958). *Le Morte d'Arthur* (1485) by Sir Thomas Malory was his primary source of the Arthurian Legend. White's conclusion, *The Book of Merlyn* (1977), was published after the author's death. These rich stories about right and might were adapted for the stage (1960) and screen (1967) as *Camelot*.

"**G**ood heavens!" cried Sir Kay. "I have left my sword at home."

"Can't joust without a sword," said Sir Grummore. "Quite irregular."

"Better go and fetch it," said Sir Ector. "You have time."

"My squire will do," said Sir Kay. "What a damned mistake to make. Here, squire, ride hard back to the inn and fetch my sword. You shall have a shilling if you fetch it in time."

The Wart went as pale as Sir Kay was, and looked as if he were going to strike him. Then he said, "It shall be done, master," and turned his stupid little ambling palfrey against the stream of newcomers. He began to push his way towards their hostelry as best he might.

"To offer me money!" cried the Wart to himself. "To look down at this beastly little donkey-affair off his great charger and to call me Squire! Oh, Merlyn, give me patience with the brute, and stop me from throwing his filthy shilling in his face."

When he got to the inn it was closed. Everybody had thronged out to see the famous tournament, and the entire

The Sword in The Stone

by
T. H. White

household had followed after the mob. Those were lawless days and it was not safe to leave your house—or even to go to sleep in it—unless you were certain that it was impregnable. The wooden shutters bolted over the downstairs windows were two inches thick, and the doors were double-barred.

"Now what do I do," said the Wart, "to earn my shilling?"

He looked ruefully at the blind little inn, and began to laugh.

"Poor Kay," he said. "All that shilling stuff was only because he was scared and miserable, and now he has good cause to be. Well, he shall have a sword of some sort if I have to break into the Tower of London."

"How does one get hold of a sword?" he continued. "Where can I steal one? Could I waylay some knight, even if I am mounted on an ambling pad, and take his weapons by force? There must be some swordsmith or armorer in a great town like this, whose shop would be still open."

> "Now what do I do," said the Wart, "to earn my shilling?"

He turned his mount and cantered off along the street.

There was a quiet churchyard at the end of it, with a kind of square in front of the church door. In the middle of the square there was a heavy stone with an anvil on it, and a fine new sword was struck through the anvil.

"Well," said the Wart, "I suppose it's some sort of war memorial, but it will have to do. I am quite sure nobody would grudge Kay a war memorial, if they knew his desperate straits."

He tied his reins round a post of the lych-gate, strode up the gravel path, and took hold of the sword.

"Come, sword," he said. "I must cry your mercy and take you for a better cause."

"This is extraordinary," said the Wart. "I feel queer when I have hold of this sword, and I notice everything much more clearly. Look at the beautiful gargoyles of this church, and of the monastery which it belongs to. See how splendidly all the famous banners in the aisle are waving. How nobly that yew holds up the red flakes of its timbers to worship God. How clean the snow is. I can smell something like fetherfew and sweet briar—and is that music that I hear?"

> "Come, sword," he said. "I must cry your mercy and take you for a better cause."

It was music, whether of pan-pipes or of recorders, and the light in the churchyard was so clear, without being dazzling, that you could have picked a pin out twenty yards away.

"There is something in this place," said the Wart. "There are people here. Oh, people, what do you want?"

Nobody answered him, but the music was loud and the light beautiful.

"People," cried the Ward. "I must take this sword. It is not for me, but for Kay. I will bring it back."

There was still no answer, and Wart turned back to the sword. He saw the golden letters on it, which he did not read, and the jewels on its pommel, flashing in the lovely light.

"Come, sword," said the Wart.

He took hold of the handles with both hands, and strained against the stone. There was a melodious consort on the recorders, but nothing moved.

The Wart let go of the handles, when they were beginning to bite into the palms of his hands, and stepped back from the anvil, seeing stars.

"It is well fixed," said the Wart.

He took hold of it again and pulled with all his might. The music played more and more excitedly, and the light all about the churchyard glowed like amethysts; but the sword still stuck.

He took hold of the handles with both hands, and strained against the stone.

"Oh, Merlyn," cried the Wart, "help me to get this sword."

There was a kind of rushing noise, and a long chord played along with it. All around the churchyard there were hundreds of old friends. They rose over the church wall all together, like the Punch and Judy ghosts of remembered days, and there were otters and nightingales and vulgar

273

crows and hares and serpents and falcons and fishes
and goats and dogs and dainty unicorns and newts
and solitary wasps and goatmoth caterpillars and
corkindrills and volcanoes and mighty trees and
patient stones. They loomed round the church
wall, the lovers and helpers of the Wart, and
they all spoke solemnly in turn. Some of them
had come from the banners in the church,
where they were painted in heraldry, some
from the waters and the sky and the fields
about, but all, down to the smallest shrew
mouse, had come to help on account of
love. Wart felt his power grow.

"Remember my biceps," said the Oak,
"which can stretch out horizontally against
Gravity, when all the other trees go up or
down."

"Put your back into it," said a Luce (or
pike) off one of the heraldic banners, "as you did
once when I was going to snap you up. Remember
that all power springs from the nape of the neck."

"What about those forearms," asked a Badger

gravely, "that are held together by a chest? Come along, my dear embryo, and find your tool."

A Merlin sitting at the top of the yew tree cried out, "Now then, Captain Wart, what is the first law of the foot? I thought I once heard something about never letting go?"

"Don't work like a stalling woodpecker," urged a Tawny Owl affectionately. "Keep up a steady effort, my duck, and you will have it yet."

"Cohere," said a Stone in the church wall.

A Snake, slipping easily along the coping which bounded the holy earth, said, "Now then, Wart, if you were once able to walk with three hundred ribs at once, surely you can coordinate a few little muscles here and there? Make everything work together, as you have been learning to do ever since God let the amphibia crawl out of the sea. Fold your powers together, with the spirit of your mind, and it will come out like butter. Come along, homo sapiens, for all we humble friends of yours are waiting here to cheer."

"Don't work like a stalling woodpecker," urged a Tawny Owl affectionately. "Keep up a steady effort, my duck, and you will have it yet."

The Wart walked up to the great sword for the third time. He put out his right hand softly and drew it out as gently as from a scabbard.

273

El Condor Pasa (If I Could)

English lyric by Paul Simon

I'd rather be a sparrow than a snail.
Yes I would.
If I could,
I surely would.

Hm, I'd rather be a hammer than a nail.
Yes I would.
If I only could,
I surely would.

Hm, Away, I'd rather sail away
Like a swan that's here and gone.
A man gets tied up to the ground,
He gives the world its saddest sound,
Its saddest sound.

I'd rather be a forest than a street.
Yes I would.
If I could,
I surely would.

I'd rather feel the earth beneath my feet.
Yes I would.
If I only could,
I surely would.

Family Emblem

In the Middle Ages, knights would wear a coat of arms as a kind of identification tag. They chose specific colors, symbols, and pictures to represent their families and themselves. Show off your heritage by making a family crest, insignia, or stamp. Interview family members about such topics as language, nationality, sports, hobbies, foods, customs, and traditions. Then come up with symbols that reveal your unique legacy.

Coat of Arms

Cardboard, scissors, pencil, glue, colored construction paper, photographs, magazines, colored markers

1. Trim the cardboard into the shape of a badge or shield.
2. Draw a horizontal line dividing your shield in half. Then draw another line dividing the bottom half of your shield into two equal sections. Cut and glue different colors of construction paper onto each section. You will now add images in each section that represent you and your family.
3. The top half can represent where you come from. Think about where you live now—are there mountains, rivers, forests nearby? Or where your family lived a long time ago—did they originally migrate from elsewhere? Another country? Then draw or look for images, like flags and symbols, to depict your family's nationality or home and paste them into the top section of your shield.

4. You can use the bottom right corner of your shield to represent favorite family sports and foods. Is there any one sport that you play or enjoy together? Look for magazine pictures or family photos to represent these sports, and you can draw or cut out pictures of a favorite family food, like pizza, and then paste them into this section.

5. The bottom left section of your shield can represent family pets or family professions. Look for a photo of your pet pooch, parrot, or goldfish if you have one and paste it into this section. Are there three generations of doctors, plumbers, farmers in your family? If so, look for images to represent the family professions.

6. Finally, draw with markers or paste the initial of your family surname into the center of your shield.

Rubber Stamp

Large rubber eraser, tracing paper, lead pencil or fine-tipped pen, X-Acto knife, ink pad

1. First, create an insignia, or logo, that represents you or your family. You might use letters, shapes, animals, or a combination of these. Keep your design simple—it will be easier to carve, and will make a clear print.

2. On tracing paper, draw an outline of the eraser. Trace or recreate your insignia inside the outline. If your symbol includes lettering, be sure to draw it backward.

3. Press the tracing paper onto the eraser and rub with your thumb so that the lead or ink will transfer to the surface.

4. With the help of an adult, carefully use the X-Acto knife to carve around the outline of the transferred image. Be sure to carve away everything that you don't want to print.

5. Press your new stamp onto an ink pad and start making your mark!

ARE YOU A GREEK GOD?

In ancient times, the Greeks saw their gods as all-powerful forces of nature. They would pray to them in times of despair and tell stories about them over blazing fires. Discover which god you most resemble.

Do you have a sunny outlook? Are you well liked? Do you do have lots of hobbies? Can you predict the future? If so, then you are like…

APOLLO. *The god of light, purity, music, poetry, prophecy and healing is perpetually young, handsome and wise. The most admirable of gods, he personifies knowledge, beauty, and perfection.*

Is spring your favorite season? Do you love plants and animals? Are you always up for a good time? Do you enjoy life? If so, then you are like…

DIONYSUS. *The god of wine and grapes, joy, youth, and cool places in spring is the protector of animal life and green plants.*

Are you always on the move? Do you like to play harmless tricks on your friends and family? Is your mind continually working on a new invention or problem? Do you like helping people? If so, then you are like…

HERMES. *The god of shepherds, travelers, thieves, and merchants is a cheerful prankster with a sharp wit. The messenger of the gods, he is never seen without his staff, winged sandals, or cap.*

Do you love the ocean and sea life? Are you mysterious? Do you have a stormy disposition? If so, then you are like…

POSEIDON. *The god of the sea, fresh waters, and horses rides a chariot pulled by dolphins and carries a trident (a three-pronged weapon).*

Of your group of friends, are you generally the leader? Do people look to you to settle arguments? Are you brutally fair and honest? If so, then you are like…

ZEUS. *The king of the gods rules the heavens and the universe. He is the dispenser of justice, protector of human relationships. Known for his wrath and for wielding thunderbolts, Zeus also is very fair and compassionate.*

CHARLIE CHAPLIN (1889–1977) will always be remembered for the original and comedic antics he performed, wearing his signature black derby hat, a ragged suit, and a little moustache, while sporting a cane. Though he came from a poor English family, Charlie made it big in America and ultimately directed his own films and even started his own movie studio. People still consider him one of the funniest and most talented actors and filmmakers of all time.

LEONARDO DA VINCI (1452–1519) created great paintings, like "Mona Lisa" and "The Last Supper." Leonardo was more than a painter, though—he was also a sculptor, architect, scientist, and inventor. He kept amazingly detailed notebooks full of things—from sketches of the human body to designs for flying machines. Anyone who is very good at many things is called a Renaissance man, which Leonardo was.

WOLFGANG AMADEUS MOZART (1756–91) is generally considered the greatest musical genius of all time. He started to play the harpsichord at age 3 and compose music at 5. When he was only 9, he wrote an entire symphony. As a young boy, he traveled from his home in Austria to play the keyboard and the violin in royal courts across Europe. This young Austrian grew up to create some of the most beloved sonatas, symphonies, and concertos of all time. His operas *The Marriage of Figaro* and *The Magic Flute* are still performed all over the world today.

HEROES OF THE ARTS

PABLO PICASSO

(1881–1973) Pablo Picasso is probably the most famous artist of the twentieth century. Born in Spain, this son of an art teacher eventually created more than twenty thousand works over seventy-five years. While most artists have one style and stick to it, Picasso went through many, including neo-impressionism, his "Blue Period," and his "Rose Period." His most famous style, though, was Cubism, in which he used geometrical shapes to represent natural forms. His passion for art also found its way into sculpture, prints, ceramics, and stage design. Pablo Picasso is often thought of as the father of modern art.

WILLIAM SHAKESPEARE

(1564–1616) was born in Stratford-upon-Avon, England, on April 23, and even though he is the greatest playwright who ever lived, much of his life is a mystery. People guess that he must have had a good education because so many of his plays and so much of his poetry are full of Latin, Greek, and classical mythology. Unlike many artists, Shakespeare was extremely popular in his day, and people flocked to his plays. Audiences today still thrill to the sound of the beautiful language and the daring action of *Hamlet, Romeo & Juliet,* and *The Tempest.*

283

Model Artist . . . Or Bust!

Do you have an eye for art? What about a nose . . . or an ear? Many of the world's greatest artists, including Pablo Picasso, Alberto Giacometti, and Auguste Rodin regularly used themselves as models for their creations. With a little papier-mâché you can be well on your way to sculpting your own likeness, too.

Shoebox, cardboard paper-towel tube, scissors, tape, balloon, newspaper, flour, water, bowl, tempera paints, paintbrushes, mirror (optional)

1. To make the frame for the neck and shoulders, cut a hole in the middle of the top of the shoebox just wide enough for the paper-towel tube to fit through. Slip the tube in the hole so that it touches the bottom of the box. Secure it with tape. You may want to cut a few inches off the top of the tube to shorten the neck.
2. For the head, blow up the balloon and tie the end in a knot. Set the knot end on top of the tube and tape it in place.
3. Prepare the papier-mâché by ripping up several pieces of newspaper into thin strips. Then, mix flour and water together in a bowl to make a runny paste.
4. One by one, dip strips of newspaper in the flour solution and cover the head, neck, and shoulders with several layers of paper.
5. To add lips, eyebrows, cheekbones,

ears, nose, chin, and hair, dip a few strips of newspaper in the flour mixture and form them into the shape you want. Then paste it in place on the bust. Try looking at yourself in the mirror as you work. Or ask a friend to model for you!

6. When the papier-mâché has dried, brush on finishing touches with tempera paint.

Bust Buster

You can turn your finished and dried sculpture into a piñata with a few simple changes.

Scissors, candy, tape, string, baseball bat or stick

1. Cut the neck off, leaving a couple of inches below the head.
2. Stick the scissors through the tube to burst the balloon. Fill the head cavity with candy. Then make two or three vertical cuts along the neck and fold the flaps against the head, closing the cavity. Tape them shut.
3. Poke two holes at the top of the head about an inch apart. Thread the string through the holes and tie a knot. Now you can hang your piñata from a tree or on the end of a pole and have your friends take whacks at it to break the candy loose!

*N*ot all pies need to bake in the oven and cool on the windowsill. These recipes call for easy cookie crusts and chilling instead of baking. You can mix and match the pie crusts with the fillings for variety. Once you discover how easy these pies are to make, you may need to have your friends over for a pie-eating contest!

BANANA CREAM PIE

FOR CRUST:
1¹/₂ cups chocolate graham crackers, finely crushed
4 tablespoons confectioners' sugar
1 teaspoon cinnamon
6 tablespoons butter, melted

Mix crushed graham crackers, sugar, cinnamon, and melted butter until well blended. Press crumb mixture into 10-inch pie plate. Freeze for one hour.

FOR FILLING:
²/₃ cup sugar
¹/₃ cup flour
¹/₄ teaspoon salt
2 cups milk
3 egg yolks, slightly beaten
2 tablespoons butter
2 teaspoons vanilla
2 ripe bananas
whipped cream

1. In medium saucepan combine sugar, flour, and salt. Stir in milk with wooden spoon and cook over medium heat until mixture starts to bubble and thicken. Remove from heat.
2. Stir in egg yolks until mixture is smooth. Cook again over medium heat for about two minutes until mixture comes to a boil, stirring constantly. Remove from heat.
3. Stir in butter and vanilla.
4. Cover surface of creme mixture with plastic wrap or wax paper so that skin doesn't form on top. Cool to room temperature.
5. Slice bananas and arrange them in pastry shell. Pour creme filling on top and chill for 4 to 6 hours.
6. Serve with whipped cream.

Makes 8 to 10 servings.

CHOCOLATE PEANUT-BUTTER PIE

FOR CRUST:
$1^1/2$ cups vanilla wafers, finely crushed
2 tablespoons confectioners' sugar
6 tablespoons butter, melted

Mix crushed cookies, sugar, and melted butter until well blended. Press crumb mixture into 10-inch pie plate. Freeze for one hour.

FOR FILLING:
6 tablespoons cream cheese
6 tablespoons peanut butter
$1/2$ cup confectioners' sugar
$3/4$ cup non-dairy whipped topping
1 package instant chocolate pudding
$1^3/4$ cup milk
whipped cream
chocolate sprinkles

1. In large bowl, beat cream cheese and peanut butter until fluffy. In two to three stages, gradually add confectioners' sugar and whipped topping and continue to beat until smooth and creamy. Spoon into pie crust and freeze for 30 to 60 minutes, until firm.

2. In medium bowl, combine instant pudding and milk. Beat with fork until smooth. Spoon on top of peanut-butter layer and freeze an additional 30 to 60 minutes until firm.
3. Serve with whipped cream and garnish with chocolate sprinkles.

Makes 8 to 10 servings.

STRAWBERRY ICE CREAM PIE

FOR CRUST:
$1^1/2$ cups Oreo cookies, finely crushed
3 tablespoons butter, melted

Mix cookie crumbs and butter until well blended. Press crumbs firmly into pie plate.

FOR FILLING:
2 cups strawberry ice cream, softened
2 cups vanilla ice cream, softened
16 ounces frozen strawberries, thawed with juice
16 large marshmallows
1 cup heavy (whipping) cream
$1/4$ cup sugar

1. Fill bottom of pie crust with strawberry ice cream. Freeze until firm (about 30 minutes).

2. Add layer of vanilla ice cream on top of strawberry layer. Freeze again until firm (about 30 minutes).
3. In saucepan, combine marshmallows with 2–3 tablespoons juice from strawberries. Stir over medium heat until melted.
OR: In micro-wavable bowl, coat marshmallows with juice from strawberries and microwave on high for about 1¹/₂ minutes or until melted. Cool.
4. Fold strawberries into cooled marshmallows. Spread mixture onto pie over vanilla ice-cream layer. Freeze again until firm.
5. Whip cream and sugar until stiff. Spoon onto top layer of pie. Serve cold.

Makes 8 to 10 servings.

MOCHA-TOFFEE ICE-CREAM PIE

FOR CRUST:
1¹/₂ cup Oreo cookies, finely crushed
3 tablespoons butter, melted

Mix cookie crumbs and butter until well blended. Press crumbs firmly into 9-inch pie plate.

FOR FILLING:
2 cups coffee ice cream, softened
12 ounces caramel topping
2 cups chocolate ice cream, softened
2 cups nondairy whipped topping, thawed
1 English toffee bar, crumbled

1. Spoon coffee ice cream into crust and spread evenly. Freeze until firm, about 15 minutes.
2. Spread half of the caramel topping on top of the coffee ice cream.
3. Spread chocolate ice cream on top of the caramel layer. Freeze until firm, about 15 minutes.
4. Spread the remaining caramel topping on top of the pie. Arrange dollops of whipped topping in a circular pattern on top of the caramel layer and sprinkle with crumbled toffee bar. Freeze pie until firm, at least 5 hours.
5. Allow pie to stand at room temperature at least 15 minutes before serving.

Makes 8 to 10 servings.

THE OAK

by Alfred Tennyson

Live thy Life,
Young and old,
Like yon oak,
Bright in spring,
Living gold;

Summer-rich
Then; and then
Autumn-changed,
Soberer-hued
Gold again.

All his leaves
Fallen at length,
Look, he stands,
Trunk and bough,
Naked strength.

Glass Garden

What if you could explore a rain forest or check out a desert landscape—without ever leaving your room? You can if you build a terrarium. All you need to get started is a goldfish bowl or a fish tank and you can capture a mini ecosystem. Take some time to learn about the plants you'd like to grow, so you can be sure you're giving them the right kind of soil and light. The reptile area of your local zoo or a nearby botanical garden can be a great place to get ideas.

Marbles or pebbles, large glass container, charcoal (from aquarium or pet shop), potting soil, decorative rocks and figurines (optional), Plexiglas lid (optional)

1. Place a layer of pebbles about 2 inches deep in the glass container to allow for good drainage.
2. Cover the pebbles with a layer of charcoal. This helps keep the soil "sweet." Then add a few inches of potting soil. *Tip: If you add a few worms to the soil, they'll make food for the plants and add life to your terrarium! If you're planning an arid landscape, choose soil that is sand based.*
3. Arrange small plants, decorative rocks, and figurines. Depending on the types of plants you choose, temperature and water requirements will vary.
4. When the plants get too big, ask an adult to help you transplant them outdoors, and start anew!

DESERT Cacti and succulents usually thrive on plenty of light and dry heat. Water is still important, but add it very sparingly—about once every month or two months should be sufficient.

TROPICAL Orchids and carnivorous plants generally like a warm, humid atmosphere. You can create a more controlled environment by covering the terrarium with a Plexiglas lid. This will recycle the water and allow condensation to build up on the sides of the glass.

WOODLAND Bark, moss varieties, and many ferns do well in cooler, shady conditions. Indirect light is often ideal. These plants like water, but if you see condensation building up on the glass, you'll know you're giving them too much.

KNOCK, KNOCK!

Knock, knock!
> Who's there?

Manuel.
> Manuel who?

Manuel be sorry if you don't open up quick!

Knock, knock!
> Who's there?

Sherwood.
> Sherwood who?

Sherwood like to come in.

Knock, knock!
        Who's there?

Harry.
        Harry who?

Harry up and open up!

Knock, knock!
        Who's there?

Lewis.
        Lewis who?

Lewis my keys and can't get in.

Knock, knock!
        Who's there?

Matthew.
        Matthew who?

Matthews are wet, can I come in and dry them?

WHO'S THERE?

IDIOMS

An idiom is a figurative expression, used in a particular language, that only makes sense within the context of its entire sentence.

A chip on one's shoulder "You have a chip on your shoulder" means that you are harboring resentment or hostility, or are overly sensitive over a shortcoming.

An arm and a leg "This costs an arm and a leg" means that the item costs a large amount of money.

All ears "I'm all ears" means that I am giving you my undivided attention.

All thumbs "I'm all thumbs" means that I'm clumsy, not very good with my hands.

Beat around the bush "Don't beat around the bush" means to get directly to the point.

Biting off more than one can chew "You're biting off more than you can chew" means you are trying to deal with too big a responsibility—or too many things—at once.

What do these idioms mean?

- At the drop of a hat • His bark is worse than his bite • Bend over backwards •
- Call it quits • Can of Worms • Dance to a different drummer • Far cry •
- Face the music • Get a move on • Hands are tied • If worst comes to worst •
- Land on one's feet • Make fun of • Off the deep end • Pain in the neck •
- Raining cats and dogs • Tail between one's legs • Up one's sleeve •
- Don't waste your breath • You're telling me •

PALINDROMES

A palindrome is a word that is spelled the same way backward and forward:

civic	madam	radar
dad	mom	refer
deed	noon	reviver
did	nun	rotor
eve	peep	stats
ewe	pop	tat
eye	pullup	toot
kayak	pup	tot
level	racecar	wow

Can you create a sentence that is a palindrome? These sentence can be read backwards and forwards. Here's are some examples:

> Was it a car or a cat I saw?
>
> Step on no pets.
>
> Rise to vote, sir.
>
> Madam, I'm Adam.
>
> Never odd or even.
>
> Too bad, I hid a boot.

One of the most famous palindromes is "A man, a plan, a canal—Panama!" by Leigh Mercer, 1914.

Word Fun!

Along the banks of the Hudson River, near Tarrytown, New York, sits the small village of Sleepy Hollow. Its inhabitants, primarily Dutch colonists, are a superstitious lot. They often spend their evenings sharing stories of the resident ghouls and goblins of their drowsy town. Sleepy Hollow's newest member, gawky Ichabod Crane, has come to town to teach the children. He often finds himself listening to their marvelous stories. The favorite and most ghastly story of all is that of the Headless Horseman. It is said that the horrific ghost rides through town after dark in search of his missing head! One evening at a country ball, Ichabod unsuccessfully woos the girl of his fancy, Katrina Van Tassel. Dejected, he mounts his horse, Gunpowder, and decides to head home. . . . Washington Irving (1783–1859) wrote *The Legend of Sleepy Hollow* in 1820. It was originally published as the sixth installment of Irving's *The Sketch Book of Geoffrey Crayon*, Gent., and became an instant classic. *The Sketch Book* also included Irving's celebrated tale "Rip Van Winkle" (1819). These stories, set in early-nineteenth-century rural America, were fashioned from German folktales. They were the first American works to gain international fame.

It was the very witching time of night that Ichabod, heavy-hearted and crest-fallen, pursued his travel homewards, along the sides of the lofty hills which rise above Tarry Town, and which he had traversed so cheerily in the afternoon. The hour was as dismal as himself. Far below him, the Tappan Zee spread its dusky and indistinct waste of waters, with here and there the tall mast of a sloop riding quietly at anchor under the land. In the dead hush of midnight he could even hear the barking of the watch-dog from the opposite shore of the Hudson; but it was so vague and faint as only to give an idea of his distance from this faithful companion of man. Now and then, too, the long-drawn crowing of a cock, accidentally awakened, would sound far, far off, from some farm-house away among the hills—but it was like a dreaming sound in his car. No signs of life occurred near him, but occasionally the melancholy chirp of a cricket, or perhaps the guttural twang of a bull-frog, from a neighboring marsh, as if sleeping uncomfortably, and turning suddenly in his bed.

All the stories of ghosts and goblins that he had heard in the afternoon, now came crowding upon his recollection. The night grew darker and darker; the stars

The Legend Of Sleepy Hollow

by Washington Irving

seemed to sink deeper in the sky, and driving clouds occasionally hid them from his sight. He had never felt so lonely and dismal. He was, moreover, approaching the very place where many of the scenes of the ghost stories had been laid. In the center of the road stood an enormous tulip tree, which towered like a giant above all the other trees of the neighborhood, and formed a kind of landmark. Its limbs were gnarled, and fantastic, large enough to form trunks for ordinary trees, twisting down almost to the earth, and rising again into the air. It was connected with the tragical story of the unfortunate André, who had been taken prisoner hard by; and was universally known by the name of Major André's tree. The common people regarded it with a mixture of respect and superstition, part- ly out of sympathy for the fate of its ill-starred namesake, and partly from the tales of strange sights and doleful lamentations told concerning it.

All the stories of ghosts and goblins that he had heard in the afternoon, now came crowding upon his re- collection.

As Ichabod approached this fearful tree, he began to whistle: he thought his whistle was answered,—it was but a blast sweeping sharply through the dry branches. As he approached a little nearer, he thought he saw something white, hanging in the midst of the tree,—he paused and ceased whistling; but on look- ing more narrowly, perceived that it was a place where the tree had been scathed by lightning, and the white wood laid bare. Suddenly he heard a groan,—his teeth chattered and his knees smote against the saddle: it was but the rubbing of one huge bough upon another, as they were swayed about by the breeze. He passed the tree in safety; but new perils lay before him.

About two hundred yards from the tree a small brook crossed the road, and ran into a marshy and thickly wooded glen, known by the name of Wiley's swamp. A few rough logs, laid side by side, served for a bridge over this stream. On that side of the road where the book entered the wood, a group of oaks and chestnuts, matted thick with wild grapevines, threw a cavernous gloom over it. To pass this bridge was the severest trial. It was at this identical spot that the unfortunate André was captured, and under the covert of those chestnuts and vines were the sturdy yeomen concealed who surprised him. This has ever since been considered a haunted stream, and fearful are the feelings of the schoolboy who has to pass it alone after dark.

As he approached the stream, his heart began to thump; he summoned up, however, all his resolution, gave his horse half a score of kicks in the ribs, and attempted to dash briskly across the bridge; but instead of starting forward, the perverse old animal made a lateral movement, and ran broadside against the fence. Ichabod, whose fears increased with the delay, jerked the reins on the other side, and kicked lustily with the contrary foot: it was all in vain; his steed started, it is true, but it was only to plunge to the opposite side of the road into a thicket of brambles and alder bushes. The schoolmaster now bestowed both whip and heel upon the starveling ribs

> This has
> ever since
> been considered
> a haunted
> stream.

of old Gunpowder, who dashed forward, snuffling and snorting, but came to a stand just by the bridge, with a suddenness that had nearly sent his rider sprawling over his head. Just at this moment a plashy tramp by the side of the bridge caught the sensitive ear of Ichabod. In the dark shadow of the grove, on the margin of the brook, he beheld something huge, misshapen, black, and towering. It stirred not, but seemed gathered up in the gloom, like some gigantic monster ready to spring upon the traveler.

The hair of the affrighted pedagogue rose upon his head with terror. What was to be done? To turn and fly was now too late; and besides, what chance was there of escaping ghost or goblin, if such it was, which could ride upon the wings of the wind? Summoning up, therefore, a show of courage, he demanded in stammering accents—"Who are you?" He received no reply. He repeated his demand in a still more agitated voice. Still there was no answer. Once more he cudgelled the sides of the inflexible Gunpowder, and, shutting his eyes, broke forth with involuntary fervor into a psalm-tune. Just then the shadowy object of alarm put itself in motion, and, with a scramble and a bound, stood at once in the middle of the road. Though the night was dark and dismal, yet the form of the unknown might now in some degree be ascertained. He appeared to be a horseman of large dimensions, and

> The schoolmaster now bestowed both whip and heel upon the starveling ribs of old Gunpowder, who dashed forward, snuffling and snorting.

mounted on a black horse of powerful frame. He made no offer of molestation or sociability, but kept aloof on one side of the road, jogging along on the blind side of old Gunpowder, who had now got over his fright and waywardness.

Ichabod, who had no relish for this strange midnight companion, now quickened his steed, in hopes of leaving him behind. The stranger, however, quickened his horse to an equal pace. Ichabod pulled up, and fell into a walk, thinking to lag behind,—the other did the same. His heart began to sink within him; he endeavored to resume his psalm-tune, but his parched tongue clove to the roof of his mouth, and he could not utter a stave. There was something in the moody and dogged silence of this pertinacious companion, that was mysterious and appalling. It was soon fearfully accounted for. On mounting a rising ground, which brought the figure of his fellow traveler in relief against the sky, gigantic in height, and muffled in a cloak, Ichabod was horror-struck, on perceiving that he was headless!—but his horror was still more increased, on observing that the head, which should have rested on his shoulders, was carried before him on the pommel of the saddle: his terror rose to desperation; he rained a shower of kicks and blows upon Gunpowder, hoping, by a sudden movement, to give his companion the slip,—but the spectre started full jump with him. Away then they dashed, through thick and thin; stones flying, and sparks flashing at every bound. Ichabod's flimsy garments fluttered in the air, as he stretched his long lank body away over his horse's head, in the eagerness of his flight.

> Ichabod was horror-struck, on perceiving that he was headless!

They had now reached the road which turns off to Sleepy Hollow; but Gunpowder, who seemed possessed with a demon, instead of keeping up it, made an opposite turn, and plunged headlong downhill to the left. This road leads through a sandy hollow, shaded by trees for about a quarter of a mile, where it crosses the bridge famous in goblin story, and just beyond swells the green knoll on which stands the whitewashed church.

As yet the panic of the steed had given his unskillful rider an apparent advantage in the chase; but just as he had got halfway through the hollow, the girths of the saddle gave way, and he felt it slipping from under him. He seized it by the pommel, and endeavored to hold it firm, but in vain; and had just time to save himself by clasping old Gunpowder round the neck, when the saddle fell to the earth, and he heard it trampled underfoot by his pursuer. For a moment, the terror of Hans Van Ripper's wrath passed across his mind—for it was his Sunday saddle; but this was no time for petty fears; the goblin was hard on his haunches; and (unskillful rider that he was!) he had much ado to maintain his seat; sometimes slipping on one side, sometimes on another, and sometimes jolted on the high ridge of his horse's backbone, with a violence that he verily feared would cleave him asunder.

An opening in the trees now cheered him with the hopes that the church-bridge was at hand. The wavering reflection of a silver star in the bosom of the brook told him that he was not mistaken. He saw the wall of the church dimly glaring under the trees beyond. "If I can but reach that bridge," thought Ichabod, "I am safe." Just then he heard the black steed panting and blowing close behind him; he even fancied that he felt his hot breath. Another convulsive kick in the ribs, and old Gunpowder sprang upon the bridge; he thundered over the resounding planks; he gained the opposite side; and now Ichabod cast a look behind to see if his pursuer should vanish, according to rule, in a flash of fire and brimstone. Just then he saw the goblin rising in his stirrups, and in the very act of hurling his head at him. Ichabod endeavored to dodge the horrible missile, but too late. It encountered his cranium with a tremendous crash,—he was tumbled headlong into the dust, and Gunpowder, the black steed, and the goblin rider, passed by like a whirlwind.

> "If I can but reach that bridge," thought Ichabod, "I am safe."

The next morning the old horse was found without his saddle, and with the bridle under his feet, soberly cropping the grass at his master's gate. Ichabod did not make his appearance at breakfast;—dinner-hour came, but no Ichabod. The boys assembled at the schoolhouse, and strolled idly about the banks of the brook; but no schoolmaster. Hans Van Ripper now began to feel some uneasiness about the fate of poor Ichabod, and his saddle. An inquiry was set on foot, and after diligent investigation they came upon his traces. In one part of the road leading to the church was found the saddle trampled in the dirt; the tracks of horses' hoofs deeply dented in the road, and evidently at furious speed, were traced to the bridge, beyond which, on the bank of a broad part of the brook, where the water ran deep and black, was found the hat of the unfortunate Ichabod, and close beside it a shattered pumpkin.

The brook was searched, but the body of the schoolmaster was not to be discovered.

Skeletons, Sorcerers and Spooks:
SPINE-TINGLING TRIVIA

1. What is a doppelganger?

2. What is the best way to bury vampires?

3. Who was the hydra, and who defeated it?

4. What is the name given to cloaked skeleton that personifies Death and carries a scythe and hourglass?

5. What are ghosts called in the tradition of voodoo?

6. Why do we commonly associate crows with death?

7. What type of sorcery involves conjuring the spirits of the dead in order to see into and influence the future?

8. How did pit vipers get their name, and where do they store their fangs when they are not striking their prey?

9. Which modern-day house pet was considered by some ancient civilizations to be the vilest of evil creatures?

10. What creature loves silver, but shrinks from silk and salt?

1. A "ghost" that is in the image of a person who is still living. The word comes from the German *doppel,* meaning "double," and *ganger,* meaning "goer." 2. Upside-down. That way, instead of prying its way out of a coffin, it was believed the vampire would dig his way straight into hell. 3. The hydra was a mythical monster with nine heads. Each time its foes tried to injure it by lopping off a head, two more would grow back in its place. Hercules destroyed the hydra as one of his famous twelve labors. 4. The Grim Reaper. 5. Zombies. 6. This association dates back to the Greeks, whose three similar sounding words, *chronus* (meaning "time"), *Cronus* (King of the Titans and Zeus's father), and *corone* (meaning "loose crow"), have come to be related. Cronus, the harvest god, carried a sickle and is the precursor to the Grim Reaper. 7. Necromancy. 8. Pit vipers—examples are rattlesnakes, fer-de-lances, copperheads, and water moccasins—have a heat-sensitive gland or "pit" at either side of their head that helps them detect when warm-blooded creatures are near. Their fangs retract and sit against the roof of their mouths when not in use. 9. The cat. 10. A ghost.

Hocus Pocus!

Sleight-of-hand performers, conjurers, and illusionists have been fooling people for centuries. But you don't have to be a Houdini to keep your friends guessing. A few simple tricks can get you on your way to a being a master magician!

Stacked Dice

Two dice, pencil, paper

1. Ask a volunteer to roll the dice while you have your back turned. Tell him or her to stack one die on top of the other.
2. Ask, "Got it?" and turn around to make sure the dice are stacked. Quickly note the number on top of the stack and subtract this number from fourteen. Say, "Good," and turn your back once again to the volunteer.
3. Keeping your back to the volunteer, write the result of your subtraction on a slip of paper, fold it, and place it on the table. Then tell your volunteer that there are three sides of the dice that cannot be seen: the one facing the table, and the two sides that are facing each other. Ask him or her to peek at each hidden side and add those three numbers together.
4. Ask the volunteer to tell you the total. Then have him or her unfold the paper you placed on the table. The numbers will be the same!

X Marks the Spot

*Two identical felt-tip pens,
old paperback book, paper*

1. To prepare, first leave the lid off one of the felt pens until it dries out. Then flip to the middle of the book and find a full page of text. Mark a big, sloppy *X* on the page with the working felt pen. Make sure the intersection of the lines clearly falls on a single word. Note that word.
2. When you are ready to perform the trick, announce that you will demonstrate your amazing extrasensory abilities. Ask for a volunteer to hold the book behind his or her back and flip it open to a page somewhere in the middle of the book. Hand your volunteer the pen that doesn't work and tell him or her to draw a large *X* on the open page while still holding the book behind his or her back.
3. Have the volunteer close the book. Then take a moment to "concentrate" on the word intersected by the *X*. Write that word on a piece of paper and hand it to the volunteer.
4. Ask your volunteer to find the page in the book marked with the X and tell you the word crossed by the X. They will find the X you made earlier with the working pen. Then have the volunteer read what you wrote on the paper. It's the same word!

H o c u s   P o c u s !

Magic Fingers

Two nickels

1. Tell your friends you have magic fingers.
2. Lay one nickel heads up on the table and let each person try to balance the second nickel on it. It will be hard to do.
3. Wiggle your fingers and tell your friends to step aside. Then lay a nickel tails up on the table. Balance the edge of the second nickel across the two middle columns of the Monticello building. (Practice this before performing the trick.)

Magic Fingers II

One raw egg

1. Tell your friends you have magic fingers.
2. Let your friends try to balance the egg on its end on a table. It will be hard to do!
3. Wiggle your fingers and tell your friends to step aside. Take the egg and shake it hard in the air for a while. (You can close your eyes and mumble some magic words while you do this.) You need to shake the egg until the white and the yolk are mixed.
4. Balance the egg. (Practice this with another egg before performing the trick. Your chances of balancing an egg are good when the yolk is broken and settled on the bottom of the egg.)

Disappearing Penny

One penny, a glass of water, handkerchief

1. Out of your audience's sight, place a penny in the palm of a hand and a glass of water on top of it. The penny should look like it is IN the glass of water.
2. Tell your audience you can make a penny disappear. Show them the glass of water, then cover the glass with the handkerchief. Say the magic words.
3. Have a volunteer take the glass from your hand and remove the handkerchief. The penny will be gone. (The trick is to fold your hand quickly over the penny when your friend takes the glass.)

"**Didaskaleinphobia**," Billy said. "It's called a fear of school. And **bibliophobia**—the fear of books — I'm sure I have that too." But then at dinner, Billy said, "Sorry Mom, no veggies, **Lachanophobia**." The little boy cried, "they really make me edgy." "Go help your sister with homework!" Mommy said, her head awhirl. "Oh no," Billy whimpered. **"What's the phobia for girls?"**

13 IFEARAPHOBIA

ABLUTOPHOBIA
Fear of bathing or washing

COULROPHOBIA
Fear of clowns

AGORAPHOBIA
Fear of crowded spaces

ARITHMOPHOBIA
Fear of numbers

ASTRAPHOBIA
Fear of thunder
and lightning

AVIOPHOBIA
Fear of flying

BUFONOPHOBIA
Fear of toads

BIBLIOPHOBIA
Fear of books

CACOPHOBIA
Fear of ugliness

CHAETOPHOBIA
Fear of hair

CHIONOPHOBIA
Fear of snow

DENDROPHOBIA
Fear of trees

DIDASKALEINPHOBIA
Fear of going to school

EISOPTROPHOBIA
Fear of mirrors

GELIOPHOBIA
Fear of laughter

HOMICHLOPHOBIA
Fear of fog

ICHTHYOPHOBIA
Fear of fish

LACHANOPHOBIA
Fear of vegetables

OPHIDIOPHOBIA
Fear of snakes

PAPYROPHOBIA
Fear of paper

PEDIOPHOBIA
Fear of dolls

SELACHOPHOBIA
Fear of sharks

TAPHEPHOBIA
Fear of being buried alive

TAUROPHOBIA
Fear of bulls

TRISKAIDEKAPHOBIA
Fear of the number 13.

XANTHOPHOBIA
Fear of the color yellow

Supervillians!

*T*hey are the ones you know and love. From
the all-powerful might of the cosmos-
roaming Galactus to the world-domineering
ambitions of Dr. Doom, they come in all
shapes and sizes, and sometimes even
with an extra pair of arms or two,
because who couldn't use a spare pair
of hands to create chaos?

THE ABOMINATION

The Abomination originates as a spy
named Emil Blonsky who manages to
penetrate the Air Force base that
houses Dr. Bruce Banner's gamma-ray
research. Blonsky stumbles upon
Banner's gamma-ray machine, exposing
himself to the ray's effects. The gamma
radiation is so strong and concentrated
(more than the radiation that transforms
the Hulk) it changes him into a monster.
He is now doomed to walk the earth as a
hateful, scaly, superhuman creature. The
Abomination's incredible strength and

stamina rivals that of his greatest nemesis, the Hulk. Unlike the Hulk, the Abomination retains his intellect.

DR. DOOM

As a college classmate of Reed Richards (later Mr. Fantastic), Victor Von Doom is an equally brilliant but arrogant scientist who becomes hideously disfigured by an explosion. Masked by a metal faceplate and impenetrable body armor, Dr. Doom takes control of his homeland, the small European country of Latveria. Not content with one nation, his ultimate aspiration is world domination. In his armor, which incorporates a force field and concussion beams, Dr. Doom can lift about 2 tons. The ability to switch minds with others is his only superpower, which he seldom uses; he more than makes up for this, however, with his enormous arsenal of cutting-edge weaponry.

DR. OCTOPUS

Brilliant atomic scientist Otto Octavius invents a tool to help him in his lab—four robotic tentacles, with claws, that are as fast as whips, strong as jackhammers, and made of steel. His colleagues dub him "Dr. Octopus" when he wears them attached to his torso. But when a freak accident fuses the tentacles to his body and gives him telepathic control over them, Dr. Octopus forgets all about scientific research and devotes his life to riches, crime, and the defeat of his enemy, Spiderman.

GALACTUS

Before there is Galactus, there is Galan, a citizen of the planet Taa. When this race of knowledge-seeking beings is destroyed by radiation, only Galan survives. The almighty power of the universe reaches out to him and transforms him into Galactus, a being with godlike, unlimited powers and the ability to channel all the energy in the universe for his use. Unfortunately, Galactus must travel through the cosmos devouring entire civilizations in order to survive.

Supervillians!

GREEN GOBLIN

An accident involving an untested, experimental formula grants Norman Osborn---
ruthless co-owner of a leading chemical-
manufacturing enterprise—superhuman
strength, a heightened intellect, and an
accelerated healing factor. Outfitting himself with Pumpkin Bombs and a gravity-
defying Goblin-Glider, Osborn, a.k.a. the
Green Goblin, embarks on a crime spree.
He becomes fixated with killing the wise-
cracking, wall-crawling superhero known
as "Spiderman" thinking he will then
attain instant credibility among the citizens of the underworld. After he discovers
the hero's true identity---college student
Peter Parker, who also is Osborn's son
Harry's best friend---Green Goblin uses
this information to terrorize Peter Parker's
friends and loved ones. He is Spiderman's
greatest enemy.

    Green Goblin's arsenal includes
incendiary grenades cast in the form of
miniature jack-o'-lanterns; smoke- and
gas-emitting bombs; a high-flying Goblin
Glider, and gloves capable of discharging
electrical pulses of up to 10,000 volts. The
Green Goblin also develops a gas that can
neutralize Spiderman's early-warning danger sense for a limited period.

THE JOKER

Little is known about the man who
becomes the Joker. A failed stand-up comedian learns of his wife's death in a freakish
accident and gets involved in a robbery at
the chemical corporation where he works.
When confronted by Batman, he dives into
a river of chemical waste and emerges a
different man---his skin is chalk white, his
lips a shocking red, and his hair a mon-
strous green. The sight of it drives him
mad, and soon Gotham City's most promi-
nent citizens are laughing themselves to
death, with a permanent smile. Batman's
most diabolical nemesis emerges.

Supervillians!

LEX LUTHOR

Lex Luthor, warped to the core, is Superman's lifelong nemesis. The source of Luthor's enmity begins in Smallville when they are teenagers. Says Superman, "My arch-enemy, Luthor, might have been the world's greatest benefactor! But he lost his hair in an accidental explosion and blamed me for his baldness! In his bitterness he became Earth's most evil criminal scientist!"

As evil as he is brilliant, Luthor carries out his villainous plots from any number of secret hideouts. Superman foils plot after plot, earning Luthor's undying hatred.

The Road
Not Taken

by Robert Frost

Two roads diverged in a yellow wood,

And sorry I could not travel both
And be one traveler, long I stood
And looked down one as far as I could
To where it bent in the undergrowth;

Then took the other, as just as fair,
And having perhaps the better claim,
Because it was grassy and wanted wear;
Though as for that, the passing there
Had worn them really about the same,

And both that morning equally lay
In leaves no step had trodden black.
Oh, I kept the first for another day!
Yet knowing how way leads on to way,
I doubted if I should ever come back.

I shall be telling this with a sigh
Somewhere ages and ages hence:
Two roads diverged in a wood, and I—
I took the one less traveled by,
And that has made all the difference.

The Chronicles of Narnia is widely considered the finest fantasy series in all of children's literature. Clive Staples Lewis (1898-1963) wrote its seven volumes over the span of seven years (1950-1956). The first and most enduring book in the series, *The Lion, the Witch, and the Wardrobe* (1950), is actually the second in the story's chronology. Book 1, *The Magician's Nephew*, was not published until 1955 but serves as the series' prequel. The story is set in the English countryside during World War II. The four Pevensie children—Peter, Susan, Edmund, and Lucy—have come to the home of an old professor to escape the bombing raids in London. One rainy day, the children amuse themselves playing hide-and-seek. Lucy hides in a magical wardrobe and discovers a "door" to the enchanted world of Narnia. Her siblings distrust Lucy's story about the snow-covered land she claims to have visited. But Edmund joins his sister on her second voyage into Narnia and sees that it is real. When the two are separated, Edmund runs into the Snow Queen—Narnia's White Witch!

"**B**ut what are you?" said the Queen again. "Are you a great overgrown dwarf that has cut off its beard?"

"No, your Majesty," said Edmund, "I never had a beard, I'm a boy."

"A boy!" said she. "Do you mean you are a Son of Adam?"

Edmund stood still, saying nothing. He was too confused by this time to understand what the question meant.

"I see you are an idiot, whatever else you may be," said the Queen. "Answer me, once and for all, or I shall lose my patience. Are you human?"

"Yes, your Majesty," said Edmund.

"And how, pray, did you come to enter my dominions?"

"Please, your Majesty, I came in through a wardrobe."

"A wardrobe? What do you mean?"

"I—I opened a door and just found myself here, your Majesty," said Edmund.

"Ha!" said the Queen, speaking more to herself than to him. "A door. A door from the world of men! I have heard of such things. This may wreck all. But he is only one, and he is easily dealt with." As she spoke these words she rose from her seat and looked Edmund full in the face, her eyes flaming; at the

The Lion, The Witch and the Wardrobe

by C. S. Lewis

same moment she raised her wand. Edmund felt sure that she was going to do something dreadful but he seemed unable to move. Then, just as he gave himself up for lost, she appeared to change her mind.

"My poor child," she said in quite a different voice, "how cold you look! Come and sit with me here on the sledge and I will put my mantle round you and we will talk."

Edmund did not like this arrangement at all but he dared not disobey; he stepped onto the sledge and sat at her feet, and she put a fold of her fur mantle round him and tucked it well in.

"Perhaps something hot to drink?" said the Queen. "Should you like that?"

"Yes please, your Majesty," said Edmund, whose teeth were chattering.

Edmund felt sure that she was going to do something dreadful but he seemed unable to move.

The Queen took from somewhere among her wrappings a very small bottle which looked as if it were made of copper. Then, holding out her arm, she let one drop fall from it onto the snow beside the sledge. Edmund saw the drop for a second in midair, shining like a diamond. But the moment it touched the snow there was a hissing sound and there stood a jeweled cup full of something that steamed. The dwarf immediately took this and handed it to Edmund with a bow and a smile; not a very nice smile. Edmund felt much better as he began to sip the hot drink. It was something he had never tasted before, very sweet and foamy and creamy, and it warmed him right down to his toes.

"It is dull, Son of Adam, to drink without eating," said the Queen presently. "What would you like best to eat?"

"Turkish Delight, please, your Majesty," said Edmund.

The Queen let another drop fall from her bottle onto the snow, and instantly there appeared a round box, tied with green silk ribbon, which, when opened, turned out to contain several pounds of the best Turkish Delight. Each piece was sweet and light to the very center and Edmund had never tasted anything more delicious. He was quite warm now, and very comfortable.

While he was eating the Queen kept asking him questions. At first Edmund tried to remember that it is rude to speak with one's mouth full, but soon he forgot about this and thought only of trying to shovel down as much Turkish Delight as he could, and the more he ate the more he wanted to eat, and he never asked himself why the Queen should be so inquisitive. She got him to tell her that he had one brother and two sisters, and that one of his sisters had already been in Narnia and had met a Faun there, and that no one except himself and his brother and his sisters knew anything about Narnia. She seemed especially interested in the fact that there were four of them, and kept on coming back to it. "You are sure there are just four of you?" she asked. "Two Sons of Adam and two Daughters of Eve, neither more nor less?" and Edmund, with his mouth full of Turkish Delight, kept on saying, "Yes, I told you that before," and forgetting to call her "Your Majesty," but she didn't seem to mind now.

At last the Turkish delight was all finished and Edmund was looking very hard at the empty box and wishing that she would ask him whether he would like some more. Probably the Queen knew quite well what he was thinking; for she knew, though Edmund did not, that this was enchanted Turkish Delight and that anyone who had once tasted it would want more and more of it, and would even, if they were allowed, go on eating it till they killed themselves. But she did not offer him any more. Instead, she said to him,

> She seemed especially interested in the fact that there were four of them, and kept on coming back to it.

"Son of Adam, I should so much like to see your brother and your two sisters. Will you bring them to see me?"

"I'll try," said Edmund, still looking at the empty box.

"Because, if you did come again—bringing them with you of course—I'd be able to give you some more Turkish Delight. I can't do it now, the magic will only work once. In my own house it would be another matter."

"Why can't we go to your house now?" said Edmund. When he had first got onto the sledge he had been afraid that she might drive away with him to some unknown place from which he would not be able to get back; but he had forgotten about that fear now.

"It is a lovely place, my house," said the Queen. "I am sure you would like it. There are whole rooms full of Turkish Delight, and what's more, I have no children of my own. I want a nice boy whom I could bring up as a Prince and who would be King of Narnia when I am gone. While he was Prince he would wear a gold crown and eat Turkish Delight all day long; and you are much the cleverest and handsomest young man I've ever met. I think I would like to make you the Prince—some day, when you bring me the others to visit me."

"Why not now?" said Edmund. His face had become very red and his mouth and fingers were sticky. He did not look either clever or handsome, whatever the Queen might say.

His face had become very red and his mouth and fingers were sticky. He did not look either clever or handsome, whatever the Queen might say.

"Oh, but if I took you there now," said she, "I shouldn't see your brother and your sisters. I very much want to know your charming relations. You are to be the Prince and—later on—the King; that is understood. But you must have courtiers and nobles. I will make your brother a Duke and your sisters Duchesses."

"There's nothing special about *them*," said Edmund, "and, anyway, I could always bring them some other time."

"Ah, but once you were in my house," said the Queen, "you might forget all about them. You would be enjoying yourself so much that you wouldn't want the bother of going to fetch them. No. You must go back to your own country now and come to me another day, with them, you understand. It is no good coming without them."

"But I don't even know the way back to my own country," pleaded Edmund.

"That's easy," answered the Queen. "Do you see that lamp?" She pointed with her wand and Edmund turned and saw the same lamppost under which Lucy had met the Faun. "Straight on, beyond that, is the way to the World of Men. And now look the other way"—here she pointed in the opposite direction—"and tell me if you can see two little hills rising above the trees."

"I think I can," said Edmund.

"Well, my house is between those two hills. So next time you come you have only to find the lamppost and look for those two hills and walk through the wood till you reach my house. But remember— you must bring the others with you. I might have to be very angry with you if you came alone."

"I'll do my best," said Edmund.

"And, by the way," said the Queen, "you needn't tell them about me. It would be fun to keep it a secret between us two, wouldn't it? Make it a surprise for them. Just bring them along to the two hills—a clever boy like you will easily think of some excuse for doing that—and when you come to my house you could just say 'Let's see who lives here' or something like that. I am sure that would be best. If your sister has met one of the Fauns, she may have heard strange stories about me—nasty stories that might make her afraid to come to me. Fauns will say anything, you know, and now—"

"Please, please," said Edmund suddenly, "please couldn't I have just one piece of Turkish Delight to eat on the way home?"

If your sister has met one of the Fauns, she may have heard strange stories about me.

"No, no," said the Queen with a laugh, "you must wait till next time." While she spoke, she signaled to the dwarf to drive on, but as the sledge swept away out of sight, the Queen waved to Edmund, calling out, "Next time! Next time! Don't forget. Come soon."

Edmund was still staring after the sledge when he heard someone calling his own name, and looking round he saw Lucy coming toward him from another part of the wood.

"Oh, Edmund!" she cried. "So you've got in too! Isn't it wonderful, and now—"

"All right," said Edmund, "I see you were right and it is a magic wardrobe after all. I'll say I'm sorry if you like. But where on earth have you been all this time? I've been looking for you everywhere."

"If I'd known you had got in I'd have waited for you," said Lucy, who was too happy and excited to notice how snappishly Edmund spoke or how flushed and strange his face was. "I've been having lunch with dear Mr. Tumnus, the Faun, and he's very well and the White Witch has done nothing to him for letting me go, so he thinks she can't have found out and perhaps everything is going to be all right after all."

"The White Witch?" said Edmund; "who's she?"

"She is a perfectly terrible person," said Lucy. "She calls herself the Queen of Narnia though she has no right to be queen at all, and all the Fauns and Dryads and Naiads and Dwarfs and Animals—at least all the good ones—simply hate her. And she can turn people into stone and do all kinds of horrible things. And she had made a magic so that it is always winter in Narnia—always winter, but it never gets to Christmas. And she drives about on a sledge, drawn by reindeer, with her wand in her hand and a crown on her head."

Edmund was already feeling uncomfortable from having eaten too many sweets, and when he heard that the Lady he had made friends with was a dangerous witch he felt even more uncomfortable. But he still wanted to taste that Turkish Delight again more than he wanted anything else.

> But he still wanted to taste that Turkish Delight again more than he wanted anything else.

"Who told you all that stuff about the White Witch?" he asked.

"Mr. Tumnus, the Faun," said Lucy.

"You can't always believe what Fauns say," said Edmund, trying to sound as if he knew far more about them than Lucy.

"Who said so?" asked Lucy.

"Everyone knows it," said Edmund; "ask anybody you like. But it's pretty poor sport standing here in the snow. Let's go home."

"Yes, let's," said Lucy. "Oh, Edmund, I am glad you've got in too. The others will have to believe in Narnia now that both of us have been there. What fun it will be!"

But Edmund secretly thought that it would not be as good fun for him as for her. He would have to admit that Lucy had been right, before all the others, and he felt sure the others would all be on the side of the Fauns and the animals; but he was already more than half on the side of the Witch. He did not know what he would say, or how he would keep his secret once they were all talking about Narnia.

By this time they had walked a good way. Then suddenly they felt coats around them instead of branches and next moment they were both standing outside the wardrobe in the empty room.

"I say," said Lucy, "you do look awful, Edmund. Don't you feel well?"

"I'm all right," said Edmund, but this was not true. He was feeling very sick.

"Come on then," said Lucy, "let's find the others. What a lot we shall have to tell them! And what wonderful adventures we shall have now that we're all in it together."

DODGE BALL

Gotcha!

Number of players: at least twelve
(an even number per team)

What you need: a large rubber ball,
a large open area to run in

Split the group into two teams. Each team stays on their side of a dividing line. The game begins when one player throws the ball across the dividing line at one of the opposing players. If the player is hit, then that player is out of the game. If the player catches the ball, then the player who threw the ball is out of the game. If no one is hit, then the other team gets a chance to throw the ball. If any player on either team touches or crosses the dividing line, they are out of the game. The game ends when every member of one of the teams is out.

Note: Since it's possible to throw the rubber ball pretty hard, it's a good idea to have a parent watch over the game to make sure it doesn't get too rough.

Fun & Games

RED ROVER

Hold on tight!

Number of players: at least eight
(an even number per team)

What you need: a large open area to run in

Split the group into two teams. Each team lines up shoulder to shoulder, holding hands. The teams face each other about ten to twenty feet apart. A coin toss decides which team goes first. The game begins when one player calls on one of the opposing players by reciting, "Red Rover, Red Rover, send [name of player] over!" The player who is called separates from his/her team, picks out a weak link in the human chain and charges, trying to break through the joined hands of the opposite side. If the player succeeds, he/she gets to take one of the players from the other side over to join his/her team. If the payer fails, then he/she becomes a member of the opposite team. The game ends when one team is out of players.

RACES

HOPPING   All of the players must hop from a starting line to a finish line. Whoever crosses the finish line first wins.

WALKING   All of the players must walk (not run) from starting line to finish line. Whoever crosses the finish line first wins. To make things interesting, have each of the players carry an egg on a spoon, a bean on a butter knife, an item on their head, etc. If a player drops the item they're carrying, they have to start over from the starting line.

WHEELBARROW   Break the players up into pairs. One player walks on his/her hands while the other player holds him/her by the feet or legs, guiding the "human wheelbarrow" to the finish line. The first pair across the finish line wins.

POTATO-SACK RACE   Each player steps into a sack that reaches up to his/her mid-section. Players hold on to their sacks with their hands and hop from a starting line to a finish line. Whoever crosses the finish line first wins.

Watch

Have you ever wondered how your watch keeps time? If you have a mechanical watch that requires winding from time to time, it is powered by what is called a mainspring.

As the spring unwinds, the two hands on your watch face move around the dial.

But how does that happen? It's all in the spur…gears—gears with teeth, that is. The unwinding mainspring turns a spur gear mechanism called a drive wheel. The drive wheel, with the aid of a minute wheel spur gear, "drives" the minute hand. The hour hand is driven by the two spur gears that are connected to the minute wheel. Together, these gears reduce the hour hand's speed to one-twelfth that of the minute hand.

But how does the drive wheel know how fast to go? The speed of the drive wheel is controlled by a mechanism called a lever escapement. A second spring, called a hairspring, swings to and fro, causing a lever in your watch to rock back and forth. The lever has pallets that hook into the teeth of the escape wheel gear. The pallets release the wheel, one tooth at a time. Then, a set of gears connects this all back up to the drive wheel. Whew! That's it!

Refrigerator

Can you imagine living in a world where cold milk, ice cream, and fresh meat were luxuries? Well that has been the way of the world throughout most of history. A reliable refrigerator was not introduced into homes until 1911.

The concept of modern refrigeration involves removing heat from an enclosed space using the process of evaporation. Have you ever rubbed alcohol on your skin? It's cold, isn't it? That's because as the alcohol evaporates, it absorbs the heat of your skin. Well, refrigerators work on a similar idea, only they use a liquid with an evaporation temperature that is much lower—it's called a refrigerant. (Never attempt to test how refrigerant would feel on your skin! It would freeze it

instantly!) A *compressor*, the motor you hear inside the refrigerator, pumps the refrigerant, in vapor form, into heat-exchanging pipes called *coils*. High pressure forces the vapor back into a liquid. In the process, the vapor gives off heat, cooling the interior of the fridge. As the coils are at the back of the refrigerator, the heat is released into the air around the refrigerator. Next, the liquid passes through an *expansion valve* at low pressure. The low pressure causes the liquid to evaporate and become cold vapor again. The refrigerant runs back into the compressor, to start the process all over.

Homemade frozen treats can rival anything an ice-cream truck has to offer. Frozen pops made out of ice cream, yogurt, gelatin, fruit or juice are delicious and fun. Leftover small yogurt or sour-cream containers make ideal molds for your pops. Experiment with different ingredients to make the perfect frozen treat. You can simply freeze fruit dipped in chocolate, nuts, or honey. It can also be as easy as orange juice in ice trays. Happy freezing!

RASPBERRY TIE-DYE POPS

3 pints fresh or frozen raspberries
2 tablespoons freshly squeezed lemon juice
1 quart vanilla ice cream or frozen yogurt, softened
Popsicle molds
12 Popsicle sticks

1. In a blender, mix 2 1/2 pints of raspberries for about 1 minute, until nearly liquid. Pass puree through a very fine sieve to remove seeds and transfer mixture to a medium-size bowl.
2. Add 1 tablespoon lemon juice to pureed raspberries and mix well.
3. In blender, combine ice cream or yogurt with 1 tablespoon lemon juice until smooth.
4. Add layers of ice cream, fruit puree, and remaining raspberries to each pop mold. Insert a knife into mold and swirl several times to create a pattern.
5. Freeze for 15 minutes and then insert Popsicle stick halfway into each pop. Freeze overnight.

Makes 12 pops.

FROZEN TREATS

CHERRY MARSHMALLOW POPS

1 3-ounce package cherry-flavored gelatin
2 cups boiling water
7 ounces marshmallow creme
2 cups apple juice
10 6-ounce paper cups
1^1/$_2$ cups mini-marshmallows
10 Popsicle sticks

1. In large bowl, stir gelatin into boiling water until dissolved.
2. Gradually add marshmallow creme and beat with hand mixer until well blended. Stir in juice.
3. Pour into paper cups. Press mini-marshmallows into gelatin with a chopstick or the end of a wooden spoon.
4. Cover each cup with aluminum foil. Carefully poke Popsicle sticks through foil and all the way into gelatin. Freeze overnight.
5. When you're ready for a pop, run hot water over the paper cups for 10 to 15 seconds to make it easy to remove the cup.

Makes 10 pops.

BANANA YOGURT POPS

2 bananas
2 ounces plain yogurt
^{1}/$_4$ cup milk
1 teaspoon sugar
6 4-ounce paper cups
6 Popsicle sticks

1. In a medium-size bowl, mash bananas with fork. Mix in yogurt, milk, and sugar until thoroughly blended.
2. Pour mixture into paper cups. Cover each cup with aluminum foil and carefully insert Popsicle sticks through foil and into mixture. Freeze overnight.

Makes 6 pops.

FROZEN PINEAPPLE POPS

10 strawberries, with stems removed
1 can (14 ounces) pineapple rings
6 ounces chocolate chips
bamboo skewers

1. Line a cookie sheet with wax paper and set aside.
2. Place one strawberry in the center of each pineapple ring.
3. With a bamboo skewer, carefully spear the pineapple from one side to the other through the middle of the strawberry.
4. Place skewered fruit on cookie sheet and freeze for one hour.
5. In microwavable bowl, melt chocolate on high for 2 to 3 minutes. Dip the top half of the frozen fruit sticks in the melted chocolate. Freeze for another hour, until the chocolate has hardened.

Makes 10 pops.

FROZEN BANANA ROCKETS

2 bananas
4 tablespoons honey
5 tablespoons chopped nuts
4 Popsicle sticks
baking sheet

1. Cut both bananas in half horizontally to make 4 chunky banana pieces.
2. Insert a Popsicle stick into the wide end of each banana piece.
3. Coat each piece in honey and roll in chopped nuts. Press the nuts into each banana piece so they will hold.
4. Place on baking sheet and freeze for about 2 hours, or until firm.

Makes 4 pops

SNOW CONES

2 cups orange juice
ice cube tray

1. Pour juice into ice cube tray and freeze overnight.
2. Put ice cubes in a blender. Turn blender on and off until ice is the consistency of snow. Serve immediately.

Serves 2.

The Rainbow

by William
Wordsworth

My heart leaps up when I behold
    A Rainbow in the sky:
So was it when my life began;
So is it now I am a Man;
So be it when I shall grow old,
    Or let me die!
The Child is Father of the Man;
And I could wish my days to be
Bound each to each by natural piety.

Stop Time

Have you ever wanted to travel in time? Suppose you had the chance to meet people who live in the future and tell them something about yourself and life in the twenty-first century. Well, even if you can't build a time machine, you can bury one! Collect items that will capture a moment in time and seal them in a time capsule that won't be opened for 10, 50, or 5,000 years.

Large, airtight, waterproof, rustproof container, such as a glass jar or stainless steel box, resealable plastic bags, duct tape, label

1. Make your time-capsule list (see suggestions on right.)
2. Once you've gathered the ingredients of your time capsule, seal them in your airtight container. Make sure that none of the time capsule contents will rust or decay. For example, paper clips and staples will rust and can damage paper items over a long period of time. For extra protection against the elements, place paper items in resealable plastic bags.
3. Reinforce the seal on your time capsule with duct tape and add a label.
4. Decide how to store your time capsule. If you bury it, be sure to make a detailed map that will let future time-capsule seekers know where to dig! Or you could make arrangements to store your time capsule in a safe deposit box at a bank. Sit back, relax, and wait for the future to discover it!

Time Capsule Checklist

THINK ABOUT ITEMS THAT...

❑ HIGHLIGHT EVERYDAY EXPERIENCES: toothbrush, article of clothing, pen, comb, chewing gum, coins, food wrappers

❑ DEPICT POPULAR CULTURE: comic book, music CD, videotape or DVD, magazine, baseball, concert tickets, television guide

❑ REFLECT TRADITIONS AND CUSTOMS: school yearbook, holiday cards and decorations, calendar that notes religious and national holidays, literature or poetry

❑ SHOW OFF THE LATEST TECHNOLOGY: newspaper articles, advertisements, printouts of Internet sites, photographs

❑ TELL SOMETHING ABOUT YOURSELF: a letter from you that includes information about yourself and your everyday life, your hopes and dreams, and predictions of the future (you might also enclose artwork, personal memorabilia, jewelry, a favorite toy or game)

Mr. Tambourine Man

by Bob Dylan

Hey! Mr. Tambourine Man, play a song for me,

I'm not sleepy and there is no place I'm going to.

Hey! Mr. Tambourine Man, play a song for me,

In the jingle jangle morning I'll come followin' you.

Mr. Tambourine Man

Though I know that evenin's empire has returned into sand,
Vanished from my hand,
Left me blindly here to stand but still not sleeping.
My weariness amazes me, I'm branded on my feet,
I have no one to meet
And the ancient empty street's too dead for dreaming.

(Chorus)

Take me on a trip upon your magic swirlin' ship,
My senses have been stripped, my hands can't feel to grip,
My toes too numb to step, wait only for my boot heels
To be wanderin'.
I'm ready to go anywhere, I'm ready for to fade
Into my own parade, cast your dancing spell my way,
I promise to go under it.

(Chorus)

Though you might hear laughin', spinnin', swingin' madly
        across the sun,
It's not aimed at anyone, it's just escapin' on the run
And but for the sky there are no fences facin'.

348

Mr. Tambourine Man

And if you hear vague traces of skippin' reels of rhyme
To your tambourine in time, it's just a ragged clown behind,
I wouldn't pay it any mind, it's just a shadow you're
Seein' that he's chasing.

(Chorus)

Then take me disappearin' through the smoke rings
     of my mind,
Down the foggy ruins of time, far past the frozen leaves,
The haunted, frightened trees, out to the windy beach,
Far from the twisted reach of crazy sorrow.
Yes, to dance beneath the diamond sky with
     one hand waving free,
Silhouetted by the sea, circled by the circus sands,
With all memory and fate driven deep beneath
     the waves,
Let me forget about today until tomorrow.

(Chorus)

349

Cheerily, then, my little man,
Live and laugh,
As boyhood can!

—John Grenleaf Whitier

Credits

"Dribble", from TALES OF A FOURTH GRADE NOTHING by Judy Blume, copyright © 1972 by Judy Blume. Used by permission of Dutton Children's Books, an imprint of Penguin Putnam Books for Young Readers, a division of Penguin Putnam Inc. All rights reserved.

From CHARLIE AND THE CHOCOLATE FACTORY by Roald Dahl, copyright © 1964, renewed 1992 by Roald Dahl Nominee Limited. Used by permission of Alfred A. Knopf, an imprint of Random House Children's Books, a division of Random House, Inc.

From THE BLACK STALLION by Walter Farley, copyright © 1941 by Walter Farley. Copyright renewed 1969 by Walter Farley. Used by permission of Random House Children's Books, a division of Random House, Inc.

From THE PHANTOM TOLLBOOTH by Norton Juster, copyright © 1961 and renewed 1989 by Norton Juster. Used by permission of Random House Children's Books, a division of Random House, Inc.

THE LION, THE WITCH AND THE WARDROBE by C.S. Lewis copyright © C.S. Lewis Pte. Ltd. 1950. Illustrations by Pauline Baynes copyright © C.S. Lewis Pte. Ltd. 1950. Reprinted by permission.

ROBIN HOOD OF SHERWOOD FOREST by Ann McGovern. Copyright © 1968 by Anne McGovern. Used by permission of HarperCollins Publishers.

"Part I, Chapter XXIII", from THE ONCE AND FUTURE KING by T. H. White, copyright 1938, 1939, 1940, ©1958 by T.H. White, renewed. Used by permission of G.P. Putnam's Sons, a division of Penguin Putnam Inc.

• • •

"Dreams" from THE COLLECTED POEMS OF LANGSTON HUGHES by Langston Hughes, copyright © 1994 by The Estate of Langston Hughes. Used by permission of Alfred A. Knopf, a division of Random House, Inc.

"Mother to Son" from THE COLLECTED POEMS OF LANGSTON HUGHES by Langston Hughes, copyright © 1994 by The Estate of Langston Hughes. Used by permission of Alfred A. Knopf, a division of Random House, Inc.

"Youth" from THE COLLECTED POEMS OF LANGSTON HUGHES by Langston Hughes, copyright © 1994 by The Estate of Langston Hughes. Used by permission of Alfred A. Knopf, a division of Random House, Inc.

"Outside and Underneath" by Shel Silverstein. Copyright © 1981 by Evil Eye Music, Inc. Used by permission of HarperCollins Publishers.

"Play Ball" by Shel Silverstein. Copyright © 1981 by Evil Eye Music, Inc. Used by permission of HarperCollins Publishers.

"The Search" by Shel Silverstein. Copyright © 1981 by Evil Eye Music, Inc. Used by permission of HarperCollins Publishers.

• • •

"Joy to the World" Words and Music by Hoyt Axton. © Copyright 1970 Irving Music, Inc. (BMI). International Copyright Secured All Rights Reserved.

"Mr. Tambourine Man" Copyright © 1964, 1965 by Warner Bros Inc. Copyright renewed 1992 by Special Rider Music. All rights reserved. International copyright secured. Reprinted by permission.

"If I Had a Hammer" (The Hammer Song) Words and Music by Lee Hays and Pete Seeger. TRO- © Copyright © 1958 (Renewed) 1962 (Renewed) Ludlow Music, Inc., New York, NY. Used by permission.

"Yellow Submarine" Copyright 1966 (Renewed) Sony/ATV Tunes LLC. All rights administered by Sony/ATV Music Publishing, 8 Music Square West, Nashville, TN 37203. All rights reserved. Used by permission.

"El Condor Pasa" Copyright © 1970 copyright year Paul Simon. Used by permission of the Publisher: Paul Simon Music.

"The 59th Street Bridge Song" (Feelin' Groovy). Copyright © 1966 copyright year Paul Simon. Used by permission of the Publisher: Paul Simon Music.

"Octopus's Garden" by Richard Starkey. © 1969 Startling Music Ltd. All Rights Reserved.

"If You Want to Sing Out" Copyright 1971 Cat Music Ltd. All rights administered by Sony/ATV Music Publishing, 8 Music Square West, Nashville, TN 37203. All rights reserved. Used by permission.

"Puff The Magic Dragon" Words and Music by Lenny Lipton and Peter Yarrow. Copyright © 1963; Renewed 1991 Honalee Melodies (ASCAP) and Silver Dawn Music (ASCAP) Worldwide Rights for Honalee Melodies Administered by Cherry Lane Music Publishing Company, Inc. Worldwide Rights for Silver Dawn Music Administered by WB Music Corp. International Copyright Secured. All Rights Reserved.

Illustrations

p. 24, 58: Jessie Willcox Smith; p. 29: Francis Barraud; p. 36: René Bull; p. 38-39: Eugene Luerd; p. 40-41: Edna Coolee; p. 64-65: Béatrice Mallet; p. 80, 176-177: Eugene Iverd; p. 86: Jenny Nystrom; p. 95: Gaffron; p. 102: H. Kaulbach; p. 108,198: H.Y. Hintermeister; p. 114, 122-123, 130-131: Frances Tipton Hunter; p. 138-139: Chas O. Golden; p. 158-159: Albin Glenning; p. 181: Torrey; p. 190 -191: C.H. Twelvetrees; p. 207: C.V. Riley; p. 212: N.C. Wyeth; p. 224: Virginia Sterretti; p. 226-227: Ernest Unterman; p. 243: William Van Drapur; p. 272: Alice Beard; p. 274-275: C.M. Burt; p. 282-283: L.P. Marsh; p. 308, 344: Ellen H. Clapsaddle; p. 313: Harold C. Earnshaw; p. 316-317: Gossett; p. 325, 328, 331 Pauline Baynes; p. 347: John Glee.